# MAGIRA

The sorcerer wrenched the door open before the priests could stop him. Then he stopped short, confronted by a wall of dark bodies, with gleaming, intoxicated eyes. He let out a shriek and reeled backwards. One of the priests tried to close the door but it was already too late.

Like a great wave the winged creatures of Darkness came flooding in. The wizard fell to the floor under the ferocity of the assault. Screams filled the temple. The beating of hundreds of pairs of wings turned the air into a whirlpool.

**Thoric watched them streaming to the altar as he turned to try to escape. But, then, with a thunderous crash the roof burst asunder. Thoric tottered, then fell to the floor as he felt searing pain as if teeth were being sunk into his flesh. . . .**

# Messengers of Darkness

*HUGH WALKER*

Translated by
*Christine Priest*

DAW BOOKS, INC.
DONALD A. WOLLHEIM, PUBLISHER
1301 Avenue of the Americas
New York, N.Y. 10019

Translation by Christine Priest.



Cover art by Jad.

FIRST DAW PRINTING, MARCH 1979
1 2 3 4 5 6 7 8 9

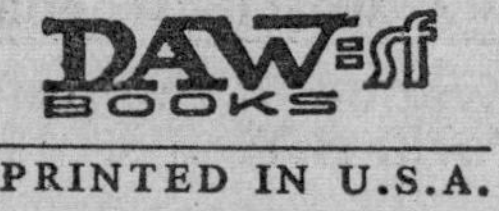


PRINTED IN U.S.A.

# Foreword

I should like at this time to explain certain of the links between the war-game and the world of Magira which may perhaps have appeared confusing to some readers. It is not of course my intention completely to blow away the veil of secrets by this demystification, however. The joy of fantasy tales, as I have already indicated in earlier works, lies in the fact that the reader may dispense with logic and scientific reasoning to share that magical, mystical consciousness with the participants. There are, however, certain things which are conducive to increasing the reader's pleasure if he is aware of them while still retaining the spell.

Meroin the historian states the year to be the one thousand and twentieth after the foundation of the legendary city of Kreos, which stands almost exactly in the center of the Old World.

Five forces are struggling for power in the Old World, five lands and five peoples that have emerged down the centuries, represented by five players who are preparing for the first decisive battle, the first game. They are the Eagle of Huascar, the Unicorn of Tandor, the Wolf of Yggrgard, the Falcon of Arullu and the Lion of Magramor. The latter has already had a part to play in the history of the Old World, in the shape of Franz Laudmann (Frankari); forces having their origins in the game itself have overpowered him, as may be read in the earlier *War-Gamers' World*.

There are six points of the compass under the skies of Magira, derived from the hexagons making up the playing surface into and out of which the pieces move. The hexagon has a magic role to play in both domains—that of the players and that of the peoples of Magira, and it has on several occasions turned out to be a door between the real world and the world of the game.

Naturally, the various peoples have differing ways of denoting the passage of time, but we propose to adhere to Meroin's records. This chronicle of the world of Magira is the most comprehensive and accurate, although even his accounts are not always of the clearest. In Magira, the year is divided into thirteen months, each of twenty-eight days. Winter consists of the months of the Eagle, the Dragon, the Elk and the Wolf, Spring those of the Falcon, the Bear and the Unicorn, Summer the months of the Centaur, the Jaguar and the Griffin, and, finally Autumn those of the Tarantula, the Vampire and the Lion. The reader may now find it easier to orient himself when the above names are mentioned.

It should be quite clear, although it is not shown as such on the map, that the Old World consists of four continents, namely Huanaca, which also takes in the islands; Ageniron, with the countries of

Moiné, Illyon, Eisatnalp, Dwyllugnach, and Clanthon; Urassu comprises Waligoi, Tuominer, Klingol, Swiatopat, West- and East-Hazzonia, and the Kanzanai, or Kanzany; finally there is Hondanan, with Taphany, Ysh, Wolsany and Esran.

For those who may be interested in delving more deeply into the subjects of the peoples of Magira, together with the cultural and political circumstances and occurrences which impinge on these novels, the Fantasy Club has published the first part of a short compendium of information under the title *Magira—Enzyklopedie*, Part 1, which also contains both maps and drawings.

Since Thoric's adventures in Kanzany are still going on, a detailed map of that land will be appearing in a later volume. I should like at this point merely to set out a brief lexicon of a few facts, knowledge of which may prove to be of use to the reader.

| | | |
|---|---|---|
| Kismah | - | the Wolsany God of Providence. |
| Sassan | - | Kanzany word meaning the devil of the air, or any sort of thief. |
| Chara | - | a port on the coast of Tanilorn. |
| Tanilorn | - | one of the four provinces to the Mir of Hondanan, the others being Timelorn, Tracy and Testar. |
| K'wan | - | Kanzany word meaning devil, often used as an expletive. |
| K'ang | - | Klingolish swear word, meaning the same as the above. |
| Arull | - | God of Evil, also an oath in Kanzany. |
| Reyah | - | Kanzany prince. |

Feast of the Sun - Kanzany feast, marking the beginning of spring.

Sea of Heaven - Kanzany name for the Sea of Perdowg.

*Synopsis of earlier stories about Magira.*

The tale has been recounted elsewhere of how, in the summer of the year 1020 after the foundation of Kreos, a strange individual, neither Yshite nor Wolsany, nor indeed belonging to any of the peoples of Magira, was found in the forests of Ysh. The manner of his dress was very odd—none in Ysh had ever seen the like. He spoke Wolsany, and claimed to know the truth of the Gods—namely, that the world was but a game for the amusement of the Gods, and men no more than the pieces in that game.

Because of this claim, he was thrown into prison by the priests of Aope, who intended to make of him a human sacrifice as a heretic upon their altar, even though this had been forbidden by the overlords of Wolsany. King Andavil, king by the grace of Wolsany, felt compelled to prevent this, while however avoiding giving the appearance of so doing. To this purpose he engaged a Tarcyan nobleman named Thuon Varth of Phelea to kidnap the priestess of Aope responsible for carrying out the sacrifice, a certain Ilara, and to take her out of the country. This was because a new priestess could be ordained only when her predecessor was dead, and the body lying at rest in the temple crypt.

Thuon, twelfth of the Varths of Phelea, was born into a long line of princes from the Mir of Hondanan, and his sword-arm commanded much respect in the courts of his own town—and he would do anything for a pretty face.

Thuon succeeded in abducting not only the priestess but also the strange foreigner, who gave his name as Franz Laudmann, but who was known to all by the name of Frankari. For both of them it was not so much an abduction as a happy escape. Ilara, who was intending to refuse to sacrifice Frankari on the altar of her goddess because of her abhorrence of human sacrifice, undertook the voyage east to Torndad with Thuon, completely voluntarily, going down the river Thar to Torndad where they hoped to find a ship to take them out of reach of their pursuers. Her hopes were however not very high, for no priestess had ever before succeeded in making good her escape, since her skin was branded with the circular symbol of Aope. In addition, she wore a ring belonging to the goddess which would not come off her finger.

They reached the soil of Tanilorn unchallenged, being sufficiently far away to be beyond the range of the powers of the Gisha, the warrior priests. Months had gone by, and all tracks had been erased.

They rested for a while in the castle of Phelorn on their way to Magramor. Frankari, who claimed to come from another world, felt that he would find a door in the south of Wolsany whereby he could return to his own world.

Bruss of Phelorn, a young man of barely twenty summers and son of General Pere who lived at the court of the Emperor in Magramor, accorded them his hospitality. He immediately took a liking to the two courageous men helping the priestess. Traces of the blood of the Mythanen, the blood of the sorcerers, flowed in his veins, and he devoted his time to the study of magic in his remote castle. He was however attracted by the lure of the libraries in Magramor and thus when Tison, a Wolsany soldier, arrived with a message from his father to say that it seemed war was likely and that Bruss' presence was desired at the Emperor's court, he was only too glad to go.

However, before they could leave, a troop of Yshite soldiers arrived at the gate of the castle, demanding that Ilara be returned to them. Their leaders were Ynnis, the King's confidant, and Peshkari, highest-ranking among the Gisha. More than a hundred men prepared to storm the almost-empty castle. Bruss was opposed even more than the others to the idea of handing Ilara over, even though it was his castle that was shortly to go up in flames. However, they succumbed to the superior forces and were taken prisoner by Peshkari, despite the fact that Bruss wove a powerful spell which carried him and Frankari off to another world—Frankari's world—but only their spirits, not their bodies. When they came to, they found themselves on a large flat surface which Frankari called a gaming-board; they were imprisoned within lifeless gaming pieces.

Bruss alone succeeded in getting back inside his own body—as a prisoner of the Yshites. For the liberation they had to thank Thoric, a Tanilorn adventurer, but before they could make good their escape, the heavens were rent asunder and a figure of legend came riding down from the clouds—the Rider of Darkness. He had come to fetch Frankari's body and carry it away to another world, a world from which emanated the fiery glow and tumult of battle, the eternal battle between Darkness and Life.

Bruss and his companions succeeded in escaping to Vanada, an ancient merchant city in the steppes of Southern Wolsany, but hardly had they arrived there than Ilara was abducted—by Daran Sorc, a sorcerer who lived in Veelgad, an ancient ruined city. She was to be the prize that he, like all Mythanen who would use the powers of Darkness, had to offer to its creatures. The scales were now weighted in favor of Darkness, and the powers of Chaos. They stormed the last bastions of life and the underlying order of the cosmos.

At the portals of the Ether, domain of the dead and the unborn, Ilara came face to face with the creatures of darkness into whose hands she had been delivered, helpless. However, she succeeded in breaking the spell and managed to escape their clutches. She came upon the Temple of Life itself, in which no living human had ever set foot. However, her very being fanned flames of passion amid the armies of Life, and they succeeded in repulsing the forces of Darkness. The scales tipped once more and soon the eternal battle was swaying in favor of the forces of Life.

Darkness fled, along with all that bore its seed. Ilara managed to escape from the Temple of Life out into a bizarre world of darkness where she came once more upon the body of Frankari, and the Rider of Darkness—and, finally Frankari himself, still prisoner of those forces which had determined to take over the body of Franz Laudmann in order to take his place in the game and to shape the destiny of the world of Magira according to their own lights.

Eventually, she once more found the door into Daran Sorc's tower, taking Frankari with her. Bruss managed to get into the tower and kill the wizard. They were still in the tower as Darkness swept it up and carried it off to its own somber realms beyond the Ether; the soil of Wolsany shook.

# 1

The cries from the shores of the lake grew louder. Dirian pushed his chair back and rose to his feet. The others at the table did the same.

"Friends," he said with a smile, "I think it has begun. Let us go on up."

A sentry appeared at the door. 'The preparations are complete, Pelarch."

Dirian nodded. The sentry bowed, and then disappeared. The Pelarch picked up his toga and put it on. His large frame was now, therefore, covered in the traditional blue fabric of Wolsany, the external symbol of the dignity and power of his position as governor of Vanada. He climbed the stairs leading up on to the roof of the building; the others followed. This particular evening there were five people dining in celebration with the Pelarch, four men and a girl. The girl was Dorana, the governor's sister, a dark-haired ruddy-complexioned creature who had soon succeeded in capturing the full attention of the men present, although the general gaiety evinced no like response in her.

The other guests were: Vardan, commander of the city guard and the Pelarch's closest confidant, a thick-set, gray-haired man from Tarcy; Thuon of Phelea, also from Tarcy, a nobleman and adventurer, whose clothing struck the oddest contrast with the simple, functional clothes of the others present—he wore a doublet of the finest imported silk embroidered in silver, and a wide-brimmed hat of the same reddish silk, with a thick clutch of downy feathers, shimmering with all the colors of the rainbow. Such finery bestowed on his solid although by no means obese form an outward impression of foppishness—indeed, it would have appeared so even at court in his native Tarcy, let alone here in the harsh Wolsany desert. However, none took offense at it.

The third man was Thoric of Chara, a Tanilorn adventurer. He was a broad-shouldered muscular fellow, with a shrewd, hard-bitten look about his face that engendered prudence in friend and foe alike. However, when he laughed, which he did frequently, a flush of boyish gaiety would wipe away the threatening expression that deterred people so.

The last of the Pelarch's companions was Goran, commander of the city guard, a dark-haired, rather mercurial Wolsany. His skin was several shades darker than that of any of the others, even that of the Pelarch and Dorana.

When they reached the roof, Dirian pointed out to them the Sea of Rhiamur, whose surface was aglitter with the lights of hundreds of torches.

"Our city has not been in such festive mood for many a long day," he stated. "But then there has not been so much reason to be merry; and if the battle had not claimed as many dead as it did—and we shall be mourning them for days to come—then they would have been able to hear us rejoicing in our victory at the very walls of Magramor itself. Such is the temperament of those who have the southern blood of Wolsany in their veins."

He signaled with his torch. The onlookers gazed in silence at the streets and the sea, where people had gathered in a dense throng. A wave of applause rose up.

Down at the wooden quay, a boat cast off and slipped slowly out across the water, dark with night. Instantly, a sheet of flame shot high into the air the length of the low gunwales. The two men who had steered the boat out leaped into the water and swam back.

As the flames licked along the length of the boat, the firelight revealed a motionless figure lying amidships.

"A state burial for a devil," murmured Thuon ironically.

"You are wrong, noble Sir," replied the Pelarch. "This is merely a theatrical entertainment, an insurance policy—and a spectacle to lighten the heart of everyone who has ever suffered the constant menace of Daran Sorc. Only now will the city be truly free of him and his magical powers. As for the insurance policy—well, that is an old but effective spell which is in common use by the forces of Life: that which fire consumes never returns!"

The flames had lit up the cadaver as if it were itself aglow, and a crackling noise was to be heard. Many present would be expecting something to occur to prevent this final destruction—many who thought sorcerers could not die, many who, in fright and uncertainty, deemed their powers to be beyond measure.

But nothing did occur—no gaping hell-hole appeared, no fire-balls shot across the water to reduce the city to ashes.

"He burns, just like any other," said Vardan in somber tones.

"And why shouldn't he?" retorted Dorana. "He is flesh and blood, like anybody else."

"I have my doubts about that," muttered Thoric.

"It is only fear which makes them appear superhuman," rejoined the girl forcefully.

The Pelarch shook his head. "He was my brother. I know that it is not merely fear. They have something of the Ether in them, it turns them into alien beings. It is as though they are simply chained to human form, and they curse it!"

"He was my brother too," the girl interrupted.

"I know that you had other feelings for him. Mythanen blood flows in your veins too—albeit merely a trace. And no matter what your feelings may be deep down inside, Dorana, the people out there are singing because they are free. It was not Daran's life they cursed, merely his ability to kill, and to make use of people."

The girl nodded slowly. "I know—I do not doubt it. But such jubilation . . . it is almost gruesome."

Dirian smiled. "It is the victor's privilege—and we have achieved a double victory. Not only have we vanquished the nightmare, but the Yshites too."

"Not decisively enough to my taste," growled Goran.

The Pelarch gave him a disapproving look.

Goran shrugged. "I say it would be far better if they were dead."

Thoric smiled mockingly. "Are you really so frightened of a mere couple of dozen men?"

Goran reddened, and clenched his fists. However, he soon relaxed. His tone was sarcastic. "Do you not know, Pelarch? The Tanilorner's head against theirs, that is the way it was put."

Thoric nodded, a feeling of unease welling up inside him.

Dirian's response was abrupt. "Then I release him from his pledge. Anyway, enough of this—too many have been killed recently. We have all achieved a victory, that is the important thing. Goran, let us have no quarreling at my table."

So saying he turned and walked back to the table. The others followed him, in tacit agreement. Goran however glared at Thoric, fury written all over his face; it was quite obvious that he, at least, was not about to release him from his pledge.

Fresh wine was brought to the table.

"When did you say Bruss is due to return?" the Pelarch asked Thoric.

"In a day or two," stated the latter. "At least, that is what he said; to my mind it may be longer. He had an idea that the ancient tower might be laden with secrets."

"He has Mythanen blood in him, has he not?" interjected Dirian.

The Tarcyan nodded in agreement. "On his mother's side, so I understood him to say." He laughed. "Are you afraid that he might take on Daran Sorc's heritage?"

"No, no—that is not the case," said the Pelarch seriously. "He would not have killed him if the blood bond between them had been that strong. It is, however, possible that he could come to some harm from learning too many of these secrets. Perhaps one day he will be able to interpret them. Then it will no longer be simple curiosity which drives him on, but that very same chill hunger which brought my brother to the state in which he now lies yonder."

"My brother is, as usual, painting things blacker than they are," replied the girl. "They do not all turn out like Daran."

"Just as long as they live in the world of men, and not among creatures of the Ether," Dirian interrupted. "I have sheltered you from such things, and I shall continue to do so as long as I can, just as long as your heart and reason remain open. But the temptations which Veelgad always held out to you have not escaped my notice. I hoped that the sands of the desert would swallow up that ill-fated tower—there is not a soul in Vanada who did not wish it so. We shall destroy it just as soon as Bruss returns. Never again shall it offer sanctuary to a demon."

"Are not the priestess and Bruss in peril out there on their own?" asked Dorana.

"I do not think they have anything to fear," said the Pelarch. "At least, not from the outside. Nobody in his right mind will go near the place."

"Tison, the Wolsany Hoendis, is on his way here with his men to whisk Bruss away to continue his journey, acting on behalf of Bruss' father. His presence is expected at the feast of Vegtis in Magramor."

"And you are going to join him?"

Thuon nodded.

"What do you expect of me? If I have understood it correctly, the priestess' fate is still in the balance, now that she is once more alive to the world around her."

"We saw her die by the lakeside, on the field of battle," objected Thoric. "I saw it with my own eyes. All the Yshites saw it. Peshkari, who pursued her out of personal hatred, is dead. Nobody but us knows that she is still alive."

"Then she should be free at last," murmured Thuon. "It was a stony road that she had to tread."

"What do you think?" Goran interjected. "Should we simply march the Yshites off?"

"That is for Bruss to decide," said Thoric coldly, "and for you, Pelarch. The attack on Phelorn falls just as much within the domain of martial law as does the battle for the city. The Emperor himself must decide. Ysh will pay whatever price is decided upon."

"Let us hope you are right," mused the Pelarch, rather less convinced. "If the rumors about the imminence of war are true then it may take place in the north, and the Lion needs Ysh to help him assemble his troops and his fleet. He is not likely to place his victory plans in jeopardy for the sake of such trivialities."

Just at that moment the walls began to tremble, and the goblets standing on the stone slab of the tabletop began to rattle. Just as they sat down once more, in wide-eyed astonishment, a white-faced sentry came rushing down from the roof, yelling: "The desert . . . the desert is glowing red-hot!"

"The desert?" exclaimed the Pelarch, jumping to his feet. "Veelgad! By the Gods!"

He went rushing up the stairs, Thoric and Thuon hard on his heels. As the others went to follow them so the palace gave another shudder, making men lose their footing, and causing a cloud of fine dust to rain down. Dorana cried out. She was bleeding. Vardan took her in his arms to protect her.

Up on the roof, they were staring fixedly southward, where the flashing bolts of unearthly lightning were lighting up the sky. Something rose into the air at incredible speed—not a solid, material body, but a long, thin, shadowy form. A third shock gave the earth to tremble once more, causing men to tumble from the roof. Screams rang out from below, and, close by, a groaning roof caved in with a crash.

Then, silence.

"That was . . ." Thuon began, and then broke off.

"Veelgad," the Pelarch concurred. "I have stared at it often enough. Something has happened in the tower, and by Arull! Those were no earthly powers at work out there!"

"To the tower!" cried Thuon. "Bruss and Ilara!" He rushed over to the staircase, and suddenly stopped. "Pelarch, give me a few men!"

The Pelarch shook his head. "I fear that you will not find any. I know the people in these parts—they know that this is Daran's revenge, and no amount of reasoning is going to fetch them out of their houses. Nobody will want so soon to ride south and confront the fury of Daran Sorc!"

"But Daran is dead. They all saw him die. They all saw his body burn."

"But not his spirit."

"Foolish prattlings!" Thuon spun round angrily.

"I shall come with you, my friend!" cried Vardan running to his side. "Let us see if we cannot get a few more men together."

Thoric made to join them, but the Pelarch held him back. "I am sorry, Tanilorner, but you are to stay here. Thoric stared at him, dumbfounded. "What do you mean by that?"

"That I have need of you here—no more, no less. I do not believe that Bruss and the priestess are still alive. I am certainly not as fearful as my countrymen, but anything might happen out there. It was your idea to keep the Yshites alive. As Goran said, you are standing bail for them . . . with your life! You are now the only one left in this city who saw with his own eyes what took place at Phelorn. They will wish to know about it in Magramor. If you want the Yshites to go to the Emperor's court, then you must remain at hand."

He let go of Thoric's arm. The Tanilorner stared at him in fury. Goran's grin broadened into a full sneer.

"As you wish." Thoric relaxed. He smiled and turned to Goran. "And what about you? What is it that keeps you within the security of these walls? Fear?" Goran's hand flew to his sword.

"Leave it where it is!" ordered Dirian sharply. "You shall accompany Vardan and the nobleman. I wish to have an accurate report of what happened at Veelgad. Although I, too, have no doubt but that Daran is dead, nonetheless I cannot but be somewhat amazed at towers flying off into the skies when they should be firmly rooted to the ground!"

Thoric's face was somber as the Tarcyan and his group of six companions left the city and headed south. But he shrugged his shoulders and dismissed from his mind the idea of simply riding off after them—the Pelarch would certainly be having him watched.

Of course, he could understand Dirian's motives to a degree, but he hated standing around doing nothing when the Tarcyan might be in need of another strong right arm.

The earthquakes had wrought considerable damage in the town. Cracks had appeared in the mud-tiled walls, and the streets were strewn with rubble. Men were scurrying about in all directions with torches. The excited cries of angry voices suddenly rang out from a side street.

The Tanilorner hesitated for a moment. The Pelarch had insisted that guests' weapons be laid aside before sitting at his table. He felt naked without his sword, but there was no time to run back to his quarters to fetch it. Trusting in his fists and the protective armor he wore under his leather shirt, he went running over toward the tumult. Despite the darkness and general confusion, it was obvious at a glance that there was a fight going on. Men were laying about one another with fists and torches. Who the protagonists were was not immediately obvious; then the throng suddenly began to bear down on Thoric. It was not until he already had his hands full that it dawned on him what was going on.

The Yshites had taken advantage of the confusion to break out of the dungeon!

Guards were nowhere to be seen. Thoric could make out about a dozen of the pale-skinned figures. They fought with fists and daggers—no swords were apparent in this game. And opposition to them was not very great either, because those attempting to block their way were the inhabitants of the nearby houses, mainly merchants and their servants, but no soldiers.

One of the Yshites seemed to recognize him, for he called something out to the others, and Thoric clearly heard the word "Tanilorner." For a moment they hesitated. Then they came at him in a rush.

*Damn it, where were the sentries?* thought Thoric. He suddenly had the feeling that he was the only one offering any resistance to the horde, and so he retreated, until the wall of a house prevented him from going any farther.

Suddenly he heard the sound of drumming hooves, coming closer, as if there were a whole troop on its way. However, it was not the guards but the remainder of the Yshites—and they had obviously given a good account of themselves for they all had gleaming swords in their hands. People retreated into houses to avoid being trampled underfoot. At least twenty horses appeared, filling the street. The Yshites vaulted onto their backs.

Thoric saw a look of uncertainty on the faces of his adversaries. Now that the horses were here every second was precious. Then a familiar voice rang out above the hubbub—the voice of Ynnis, their leader.

"Bring the Tanilorner with you—and I want him alive! And look sharp, too. Do you propose to wait until we've got the whole city up and after us?"

This spurred them on. For a moment Thoric managed to hold them off, but then he fell to the ground under the weight of his attackers, and he no longer had room even to lash out with his fists. Then they were on top of him, holding him down. He thought he was going to suffocate. He lay there half-stunned, and when they finally let go of him he found himself bound hand and foot. They lifted him into the air and threw him across the back of a horse, causing his stomach to turn over. A few moments later they had tied him on firmly, and were galloping at breakneck speed through the darkened streets, heading for the shore of the lake. Nobody tried to get in their way. Confusion reigned everywhere.

They came upon the road used by the merchants, which they followed until such time as it stopped heading north. Thoric gave up tugging at his bonds. To succeed in loosening them would mean certain death beneath the hooves. There would surely be a better way of escaping later on, and anyway, in his present highly uncomfortable position he had enough to do just trying to remain conscious.

When the road turned west they left it to ride north. They slowed the pace a little. The night was very dark, and the ground in the savannah was treacherous. The lights of the city disappeared from view. There was no sign of pursuit, and it was a certainty that nobody would be able to follow their tracks until morning.

*It looks as though they are heading back toward Ysh,* Thoric thought to himself. But why were they taking him with them? Had they found out that Ilara was not dead after all, that the burning they had witnessed had been merely an image projected by mirrors? Perhaps they were hoping to return with reinforcements? But none of these went any way toward explaining why they were taking all this trouble to carry him along with them.

When dawn broke they stopped to rest, and released him from his uncomfortable position. He was so exhausted that he fell asleep instantly, despite his bonds and the damp grass.

Shortly after sun-up they set out once more. There was still no sign of any pursuit, and Thoric wondered whether the Pelarch would do anything at all. Would he not after all be pleased to be rid of both his problems—the Yshites and the Tanilorner? What fairy tale would he invent for Thuon on his return? If indeed he did return!

Thoric bit back his fury. There was nothing he could do but just try to stay alive.

This time they attached him upright on the horse, and the ride was therefore considerably easier. Nobody would talk much to him, however, and his questions went unanswered. The men were exhausted and sullen—their time in the dungeon had certainly been no holiday! Many bore wounds received during the battle by the lake, and even Ynnis himself sometimes suffered bouts of faintness, such that his men had to support him. However, they also knew that they had no time to lose—they would not feel safe until they were once more riding through the forests of their homeland. But that was still a long way off, and much could happen in the meantime. They obviously had no intention of killing him, however—at least, not while Ynnis was still alive.

His chances were not really so very bad—after all, the Yshites owed him their lives.

Apart from casting the occasional look at his bonds, they bothered little about him during the ride.

In late afternoon, the hithertofore cloudless sky suddenly darkened. Clouds gathered in a somber mass on the horizon to the east. A breeze sprang up, causing the waist-high savannah grass to billow like a yellow sea, in constant motion. The wind was refreshing, and it gave new heart and strength to the exhausted riders. It brought with it the scent of rain, presaging the onset of the winter rain storms.

At one point, they caught a glimpse of a distant pride of lions, but the lions were more interested in a herd of marus than in the horsemen.

Finally they came upon a small depression, and in it a pond overgrown with rushes. It was a suitable place to camp for the night. There was game all around them, and as long as a fire was burning the feared beasts of prey would keep their distance. Moreover, the light of the fire could only be seen from very close by.

Of pursuit there was still no sign, which merely further reinforced Thoric's conviction that Dirian had no intention of coming after them. Thuon or Bruss might set out on the trail of the Yshites, but it would be at least two days before they returned from Veelgad—if indeed they returned at all!

Fate had decreed that he should be separated from his companions. He regretted this, but in his present situation there was nothing he could do. Still, the Yshites were not letting him starve, and the greater the distance they put between themselves and Vanada the friendlier they became toward him. True, his questions still fell on deaf ears, but they now loosened his bonds to set up camp. From time to time Ynnis' gaze would come to rest on him. He returned it calmly. He himself was muscular and strong, and he towered over most of the Yshites, but nonetheless he appeared frail in comparison with Ynnis' bear-like frame. He admired the man—and not merely because of his courage and physical strength. He had an air of imperturbability about him which permitted him to defy even the Gisha. It was the fact that he despised men such as Peshkari—who murdered and perpetrated acts of great cruelty in the name of their gods—that gave him a common bond with Thoric—and which was also Thoric's undoing, as events in Vanada had proved!

A slight noise woke Thoric up.

Something was moving about somewhere nearby—either a large animal or a man bent double, he could not quite make it out in the darkness. The fire had almost gone out, its glow half-hidden by the ashes. Thoric shivered. His arms were stiff, as were his legs, although his bonds did permit him to lie fully stretched out. On the edge of the depression he could see the outline of a sentry silhouetted against the star-studded sky. Snoring noises came from around the fire. Was that what had woken him, perhaps?

No—he saw the shadow move once more and he heard a rustle in the grass. Both were approaching. If it were an animal it would surely long since have attacked one of the men sleeping in rows, through whose midst the creature was stealthily gliding.

Suddenly he realized that he was the target. It occurred to him that there had been certain of the men who seemed not to agree with Ynnis' plans. He tensed himself. Whoever it was, he was certainly not coming to set him free.

He raised his legs and rolled slowly over onto his back. The shadowy figure had come to a halt. There was not a movement to be discerned throughout the whole camp. A moment later, the crouching form appeared right in front of him in the trodden-down grass.

He forced himself to breathe regularly as the man inched cautiously nearer. Through half-closed eyes Thoric saw the flash of a blade. He suddenly raised his legs and lashed out. Something grazed his calf, painfully, and then his attacker was whirling through the air, uttering a strangled cry.

A number of men awoke, and threw themselves on top of Thoric and his assailant. The former ceased all resistance, but the other man was not so easily subdued. It needed a sharp blow with the hilt of a sword to bring the struggle to an end.

Instantly torches flared, illuminating the scene of the fight. Thoric looked hard at his would-be murderer, who was lying motionless on his back, his face bleeding from the force of the blow. The dagger had fallen from his hand. Thoric did not recognize him. He had never met him in his contacts with the Yshites.

Ynnis appeared in the light of the torches. He gazed first at the unconscious aggressor, and then at the Tanilorner.

"Release him from his bonds!"

Two Yshites stepped up and untied the ropes. He stretched joyfully and agitated his arms and legs until the blood started to course once more through his half-numb limbs. He looked at Ynnis. It was a look of thanks.

The leader of the Yshites gestured toward the unconscious figure of Thoric's assailant.

"Tie him up. I shall decide his fate in the morning. It would seem that Peshkari is not yet dead—then I shall track down and extirpate his spirit wherever I find it. No more injustices shall be perpetrated in the name of Aope. The King's dungeons await anybody who disobeys my orders."

The men stood in silence listening to his words.

"Come over to the fire," Ynnis motioned to Thoric. "We must talk."

A couple of men began to rake over the fire, throwing some pieces of dead wood onto the embers which soon flickered once more into life. It burst into a crackling blaze.

Ynnis gave the Tanilorner time to warm his cold hands, staring thoughtfully into the flames. After a lengthy silence, he spoke: "No, Peshkari is not dead. The King was right. The gods of antiquity are cruel. They fill the hearts of men with somber and gloomy thoughts." He fell silent for a moment, then he went on: "The one who tried to kill you is Pharor—one of Peshkari's men, one of those who will never forgive either of us for not groveling on our knees before Peshkari."

Thoric nodded in silent agreement, waiting for the other to continue. "If you are not going to escape then there is no reason to tie you up," he went on. "Your word will be enough for me."

Thoric hesitated. "Where are you taking me?"

"To E'lil. You will report to the King. Peshkari's high-handed actions at Phelorn and Vanada will cause difficulties for my country. The priests will speak with their false tongue, and it will be my word against theirs. Your account may well seem very important to the King."

Thoric shook his head in astonishment. This was the second time that somebody had wanted him as a witness—firstly in Magramor and now in E'lil.

"What makes you so sure that I shall speak in your favor?" he asked.

"You will certainly not speak in Peshkari's favor, and that is enough."

"I come as a free man, I shall speak as such. After that I shall be free to go where the fancy takes me? Will you pledge that?"

"That is for the King to decide. Nor are you a free man. I would not let you escape alive while on the soil of Wolsany. But there is something that I can offer you when we reach E'lil—word of the fate of your friends Bruss and Ilara."

"Bruss and Ilara?"

Ynnis made no reply. He made to stand up.

"Wait. You have my word," said Thoric, rapidly.

Ynnis sat down once more, and smiled. His narrow eyes came to rest on the Tanilorner. His delight was evident.

"We know that it was not Ilara that Peshkari killed in Vanada." Ynnis' smile broadened. "It all looked very real, and at the time nobody had any doubt but that it was Ilara that they were looking at—not Peshkari, not I . . . not even you. . . ."

Thoric nodded. "That was Daran's doing."

"We heard about it later," stated Ynnis. "In the dungeon . . . but by then we already knew that we had been duped, that Ilara was still alive."

"How?" asked Thoric. "How could you have known that?"

"A priest's secret, Tanilorner. There could be no escape for Ilara, no way out—except death. Peshkari's myrmidons soon discovered that she was still alive. Pharor is one of them. However, when we had the earthquake, the signals suddenly stopped."

"Does that mean that she is dead, then?" asked Thoric.

Ynnis shrugged his powerful shoulders. "As far as I understood it, the priests do not know. Something happened which they cannot comprehend. Her death cannot be the explanation, for they would find her corpse just as readily, and they cannot find that either."

Thoric nodded to himself. He remembered the ring on Ilara's finger that would not come off. Even as far back as the battle for Phelorn Bruss had had the suspicion that the ring was the reason why the girl had not been able to shake off her pursuers.

But what could have happened? It had looked as though the sorcerer's tower had been destroyed by some power or other—and it had to have been a mighty power to have caused the earth to tremble so strongly that houses a day's ride away collapsed. And Bruss and Ilara had been in the tower at the time, together with the dwarf Thauremac about whom Thuon had told such strange tales.

What had happened to them?

Without so much as Ynnis' asking him to he recounted what he had learnt from Thuon about events in Veelgad; about the battle around the tower, Daran Sorc's death, and the freeing of Ilara. But in all of it there was nothing to cast any light on the impenetrable mystery, not even so much as the vaguest clue. All the secrets lay buried in the ruins of Veelgad.

"Why are we riding north if the solution to the mystery lies in the south?" asked Thoric. "Let me go back. I shall bring you news of what the Tarcyan has discovered."

Ynnis shook his head. "No. Nobody will discover anything in Veelgad. The priestess is no longer of this world."

"No longer of this world?" echoed Thoric incredulously. "Where then? Floating in the Ether?"

"Even the priests do not know. But when they are back in E'lil they will ask Aope—and she will answer them."

# 2

Fourteen days later they reached the region where lay the source of the river Vert, and they turned to ride eastward along the foot of the mountains of Taphany. No further incidents occurred. Pharor was kept under constant guard. Another Gisha and two acolytes spent most of their time congregated around him. They cast hostile glances at Ynnis and Thoric, but they made no attempts to pursue matters further. They contented themselves with merely staying away from the other Yshites. Since Peshkari's death Pharor appeared to have become their leader, and Thoric could not shake off the disquieting feeling that the last word had yet to be spoken, that the disgrace would not remain unatoned for when they reached E'lil and had the strength of the temple behind them.

At one point they came upon a Wolsany patrol who eyed them suspiciously, but they seemed satisfied with their explanations. News from Phelorn and Vanada seemed not yet to have traveled so far to the Yd.

One of the Yshites died of wounds received during the battle around Vanada, and although they had for several days moved forward only slowly on his account, still no pursuers appeared.

Ynnis was recovering extremely well despite the exertion of the endless ride.

The mood of the men improved markedly when the interminable forests of Ysh appeared in the distance. Two-thirds of the journey lay behind them, and they were now traveling through that familiar, eternal green twilight in which no enemy could hope to best them. Even the danger from the tribes of centaurs would not diminish their good spirits.

However, Thoric's uneasiness grew with every pace they took in this endless primeval forest, so far away from any caravan route.

He came to admire the Yshites, the skill with which they moved about in their own familiar surroundings, their infallible sense of direction, their courage in battle with the beasts of the jungle.

Thoric missed the open sky. It was a rare event to glimpse an expanse of it, for most of the time the green forest roof stretched away above his head.

On the twenty-fifth day they reached Orn, a pyramid of vast dimensions, built of stones of such regular shape that Thoric thought it unlikely that these edifices had been erected by human hand. They had to be of ineffable age, older even than the primeval forest which itself stretched back thousands of years; no men could have carried these gigantic blocks of stone through the forest. Great wide roads would have been necessary for such a feat.

The pyramid sloped down on three sides. Here and there narrow openings could be seen, looking like slits to shoot from. The sides soared steeply up. One could climb a little way up them, as far up as the undergrowth had managed to eat into the stone, but where one could see through the tangle of branches, the stone walls stretched endlessly away into the sky, high above the tops of even the tallest trees. They were standing on a hill. A dark opening, taller than a man, led into the interior where not so much as a single shaft of light was to be seen.

In the tiny clearing in front of the entrance there stood a few simple huts made of branches, the dwellings of some five dozen men—quite definitely Yshites, being so fair-skinned, although smaller than Thoric's companions. He learned that they were savages, hunters of whom there was always a small number in residence around the pyramids, guarding them against the centaurs. But they were not kith and kin to the ancient race, to the great Yshite people as old as the world itself, who according to legend had wrested immortality from the gods.

The half-naked hunters were peaceable. They greeted Ynnis and his men with reverence, and Thoric with glances filled with curiosity. The women were without exception taller than the men. They were slim, with flat, pendulous breasts and short hair. This struck Thoric as odd, for he had never seen women with their hair cut so short. They wore bracelets and earrings of silver, although the younger women wore no jewelry and wore their hair long, like the men. A lengthy palaver took place around the campfire—Thoric understood scarcely a word of it. He already had some difficulty in understanding the Yshites, but he could not follow the dialect of the natives at all.

The tribe laid on a small feast in honour of their guests, consisting in the main of copious eating, dancing, banging drums and quaffing an intoxicating beverage to which even the hard-headed Tanilorner was not equal.

In Thoric's hazy memory, the jungle echoed with the sounds of the singing, or rather the bawling, of several dozen voices, and it was no doubt only this howling which prevented the feared centaurs from overrunning the camp.

What Thoric did not know was that sentries had been posted around the camp, and that a number of sober guards were standing ready in the event of danger to drive the whole camp, at spear-point if necessary, into the shelter of the pyramid.

The following morning Thoric had the opportunity of seeing inside the ancient monument. Ynnis decided that a group of his men should go inside to reconnoiter, and he offered no objection to Thoric's joining them.

Climbing the damp, narrow steps proved arduous. There were many stories, each a little brighter than the one below it, for the narrow openings which Thoric had noticed from the outside filled the increasingly tiny rooms with an ever brighter light. Outside, the jungle too became more and more luminescent. The rooms were bare, except for a few animals' tracks and birds' nesting places.

Thoric came to realize that over a thousand men could take refuge in the two lower stories alone. Doors of stone could be pushed across to seal the entrances.

Up at the summit they were able to step out into the open air. The sight which greeted them left a very strong impression. They were higher up than the tops of the tallest trees in the jungle. Below them, an endless sea of gently swaying vegetation stretched away into the distance. Above them, the sky was half filled-in with clouds. A wide ribbon-like structure ran away, quite clearly visible, in a dead straight line to a point two or three days' ride distant, where, provided their eyes were not playing tricks on them, the pointed summit of another pyramid jutted up through the roof of the forest. Such ribbons radiated throughout the forest, almost like the spokes of a wheel—to the Yd, to the north, to the east and to the Mir. Only to the south and west, where there lay only the Wolsany savannah, were there no such sights to be seen. At the end of each of the spokes there stood further pyramids, and Thoric was told by the Yshites that ancient edifices of this nature were to be found all over Ysh and that, with their help, one need never lose one's way.

It looked to Thoric as if Titans had at one time created vast clearings in the forest, stretching out straight ahead, but that over the centuries the jungle had gradually reclaimed them.

Three days later they were encamped at the foot of the pyramid which they had seen from Orn. It was identical to the other. What impressed Thoric most was that there were no signs of decay. The jungle seemed unable to fasten its hand round these edifices. Thoric had seen ruins in primeval forests before, and he knew the might with which the jungle strove to overgrow once more those regions which man had succeeded in wresting from its clutches for a while.

Once more a group of Yshites climbed up to the summit inside it, and Thoric accompanied them. The regularity and order left a deep impression. In all six directions these clearly visible strips of lighter vegetation stretched away into the distance, ending in the gleaming white peaks of five other pyramids. To the east the gleam was even brighter, as though there were many buildings there.

It was E'lil, the eternal city—their journey's end.

In two or three days they would be standing before its gates. None of the Yshites sought to hide his delight. They had been on the road for many long months—more than a hundred had set out, and not more than two dozen were returning. And they had not been successful—they had lost Ilara's trail.

The whole episode had been ill-starred, even the powers of the Gods had been against them. The Rider of Darkness had come down to the earth. Times ahead were bleak.

Blood and battle. Aope's wrath would be aroused.

However, they were tired, and the joy of homecoming outweighed all the portents of gloom.

Only one of them, understandably, did not share the mood of enthusiasm—Thoric the Tanilorner. His fate was very uncertain. This he saw more and more clearly with every step he took nearer the marble temples of E'lil.

# 3

At first sight, Thoric could not discern much of the city's legendary splendor. He was astonished to see the mighty walls and palisades which seemed to surround the entire city, and he wondered what the inhabitants could be so frightened of. Centaurs? He had glimpsed no sign of them but their tracks throughout the whole ten days of the journey through the jungle. The wall and palisades were crowned with stakes. This would surely not deter human assailants—indeed, they would be more likely to help them clamber up the walls.

The greater part of the city was constructed of stone and marble—and, just as for the pyramids earlier, the question went begging: how had such huge blocks been transported through the jungle? Perhaps along those long, thin glades which might at one time have been roads, and probably out of the mountains of Taphany, which must have been a mighty undertaking. But then, all the things he had heard about Yshite legends during the ride suggested that the Yshites were no ordinary people.

As they rose up to the palace, Thoric shook his head continually. Of the erstwhile splendors there remained but little—merely stones, and riddles.

The scene was a peaceful one. People waved happily to the returning heroes, and cast glances filled with curiosity in Thoric's direction. A few moments later, however, it was back to harsh reality. The Gisha were anxious to ride off to the temple with Pharor immediately, but Ynnis had other plans for him. He was to be taken before the King, along with Thoric.

"I know that the King looks favorably on your disregard for the priests of Aope," said Pharor in a hate-filled voice. "One day, however, you will pay for your arrogant pride, just as Peshkari prophesied."

Ynnis shrugged. It was easy to see just how little this threat bothered him.

The other Gisha reached for their daggers, faces screwed up in fury; however, they realized that this was neither the time nor the place to go seeking revenge—there were too many witnesses in the street, too many who were loyal to Ynnis and the King.

*How deep must be this chasm between the King and the priests to engender such hatred,* thought Thoric.

Ynnis and his men rode off to the palace; the Gisha galloped off to the Temple. As they rode up to it, they saw that more than three dozen men had assembled in front of the temple gates, awaiting their arrival. The looks they cast in the direction of Ynnis' men promised no good.

But no further incidents occurred.

The King waited for Ynnis to arrive with impatience—his impending arrival had been announced by scouts.

The King cast the Tanilorner a searching glance, and nodded. He was a spare man, almost bald, and the skin on his scalp bore the red circular imprint of the silver crown which lay on the table before him.

It is not merely his head that is weighed down by that crown, Thoric thought to himself. The crown of Ysh was no easy burden to carry in these days when civil war looked so close and the hand of the Wolsany overlords was rattling and shaking the old traditions.

The King wore a cloak of green velvet, and he sat on a throne that had been hewn in one piece from a huge tree, adorned with the heads of ancient deities and the circular symbol of Aope, Goddess of the forest.

"I have heard Ynnis' report," said the King, "and yours too, Thoric of Chara. I do not doubt your words. I shall not try to hide the fact that since Aope's sacrificial priestess took flight the city has been more peaceful. The fact that the human sacrifice demanded by the priests has been averted has relieved me of the awkward choice between the priests (and hence the ancient traditions of our people), and the overlords of Wolsany, to whom I, as King, am duty-bound. Let me tell you that this is a choice between two evils, both of which lean heavily on forces that should not be underestimated, the priests with their Gods and the Wolsany with their armies. I would free Ysh of both of them—at least, that was my dream when I came to the throne. Ancient and bloody traditions hamper our people just as effectively as the laws of Wolsany, so foreign to us. However, I have no intention of pouring my heart out to you, Tanilorner—just enough for you to understand me, and my decision."

"Your decision, sir?" asked Thoric, with a disagreeable sensation of nervousness.

Andavil nodded. Ynnis surveyed the two of them, frowning. It was clear that he took no pleasure in the situation.

"If I am to believe the reports of my confidant," the King went on, pointing a finger at Thoric, "then you contributed in no small measure to the, er . . . very great success of the priestess's escape?"

Thoric made no reply.

"For that I thank you," the King declared. "However, events have now taken an extremely unfavorable turn. The fact that the priestess has disappeared completely bothers me not one whit—but it has happened too soon. I have to know what plots they are hatching in the temple. Lives depend on it. Whatever plans the priests might make, I must stay a step ahead of them, for if slavery is to come to the people of Ysh, then let it be to the armies of Wolsany rather than to the bloody decrees of the false deities of antiquity."

He broke off, breathing heavily, and then went on rapidly: "There is to be war . . . next spring, or perhaps even this summer. The forces of Wolsany will gather in Ysh, or the coast, at Hero Straits. I think it will happen in the north, as long as the snows melt in the highlands of Kanzany. But that is not yet certain. Once the troops are here then the priests will not dare to take any action, for then it would be plain for all to see that it was they who had caused the Wolsany to come. And it would mean the end of our complete and independent self-government. That is why they will endeavor to fan the flames, to make me look the arch-villain. They know that I would never tolerate a return to the worship of the ancient false Gods of Darkness. They also know that I will avoid civil war—at any price. They also know that if it is a matter of survival or destruction then I will call on Wolsany for aid. I shall be the devil who plunges Ysh into slavery . . . as if that had not already happened long ago! Their fanatical cult of these idols will win new adherents. However, the danger has been averted, for the moment at least."

"But . . . I do not understand . . ." began Thoric, becoming ever more uneasy within himself.

"But you must understand, Tanilorner," replied the King, "for it is all to do with Ilara, and therefore with you. You know that well enough, although it must sound more convincing and be more comprehensible coming from the lips of an Yshite. This has been a year rich in calamities for our people, indeed, so rich that skeptics might even feel that the Gods had turned their backs on the Yshites. The Thar burst its banks, bringing death and sickness down upon Torndad and the many other settlements along its course. Never have the centaurs been so aggressive in this part of the country. Every soothsayer is seeing gloomy omens. The priests are seizing on this as a reason to commit an act strictly forbidden by Wolsany—a human sacrifice. Only blood, only a human life can placate the gods who have turned their faces away from Ysh. Only blood can regain the favors of Aope. But it is not Aope they are thinking of—they have in mind the false deities of antiquity, and none can say what forces might arise as a result of such an act, even aside from the transgression of Wolsany law and the consequences of that. But now the gods have smiled on us . . . for the first time this year." He smiled. "The chosen victim has escaped. . . ."

"Frankari?" asked Thoric.

The King nodded. "Yes, Frankari the heretic, whoever he was. And with him in his flight went Ilara, sacrificial priestess to Aope—perhaps because she was afraid to wield the dagger, afraid to commit murder. Who knows what went on in the girl's head?"

It seemed to Thoric that the King smiled once more as he spoke these words.

"You must know that a priestess to Aope devotes her life to the goddess. The laws of the cult decree that only after one priestess is dead can another be ordained. That is why it is, my Tanilorner friend, that the Gisha, self-styled soldiers of the gods, pursued her so bitterly. Only with Ilara dead can they bring their plans about."

"But what about Ynnis and your soldiers?" Thoric interrupted. "Why were they fighting on the side of the priests? Surely you were anxious that . . . Oh!" He broke off, grinning.

The King nodded. "A clever trick, you must admit. Had I not done so then much suspicion might have fallen on me. Moreover, my men had lots of opportunities of hindering the progress of the pursuit whenever it seemed necessary to do so. But now that Ilara appears to have disappeared off the face of this world the priests might get the idea of simply declaring her to be dead, do you see? Thus the way would be open to find a new priestess, and a new sacrificial victim. Steps must be taken rapidly, before the armies of Wolsany can mobilize. . . ."

Thoric nodded pensively.

"Tanilorner, you shall spy for me!"

"I?" exclaimed Thoric. "Sir, how can you suggest such a thing. There are no clothes I could wear that would make me look like an Yshite, and in the meantime people all over the city will have heard that I arrived with Ynnis, that I helped Ilara and that Pharor tried to kill me. And the priests know that there is one party whose side I certainly cannot take—theirs. How by all the Gods could I discover what they are plotting?"

"You will hear much more once you are inside the temple."

"But I shall never get inside the temple."

"Ha! There is nothing easier," replied the King. "As soon as you set foot in the street they will be after you. You will be inside the temple even more quickly than you would wish!"

"But I would not wish it at all . . . anything but . . . ."

"I can understand that, Tanilorner, but I fear that you have no choice. You will leave this palace within the hour. The priests' bailiffs are already lying in wait around the palace. They will be trying to capture someone to offer in exchange for Pharor. I would release him for you. . . ."

Thoric's gaze shifted from the King to Ynnis, and then back again. It was plain to see that Ynnis was not happy about the state of affairs. The King was trying hard to reinforce the impression that his hands were tied, that all these events were not of his choosing.

Just at that moment there rose a commotion from the street. The King leapt to his feet and ran over to a window. Thoric and Ynnis followed. A troop of Gisha, clearly recognizable by the white triangular star on their helmet, were riding across the temple square. Thoric counted six of them. In their midst rode a strange figure—an old man with white hair and a white beard. He wore white clothing, with something not unlike a monk's cowl; and even from that distance his face had a ghostly look about it, almost as though it were but bare bone.

"A Mythan!" muttered the King.

"A sorcerer?" exclaimed Thoric.

King Andavil gave a gentle nod. They watched the troops dismount in front of the temple, and four of them led the white-haired old man off into the temple.

"This is not good," declared the King. "He was here before, a month ago. On that occasion he came to the palace. Only once before have I seen such a man—at the court of the Emperor in Magramor." He shuddered. "There is so little of the human about them. One has to be as cold-blooded as a fish to endure their proximity. I know that there are many who prize them as counselors and sages, but it makes me shiver to be near them. . . . He gave his name as TrondasKhyn. He did not say where he came from. He offered his services, but I declined with thanks. He must quite plainly have felt the way I look on his kind. I have not seen him since . . . until today. His going to the priests fills me with anxiety. His presence will be even less welcome to me if he is on their side than on my own." He spun round abruptly. "Tanilorner! I must know what is going on inside those unholy walls, and you are the only one who can find out."

"The stakes are damned high," growled Thoric. "I heard Ynnis say that the only way out of the temple dungeons is via the executioner's block."

"That is so, unless you have me on your side."

Thoric nodded. "Yes, that I see. What is not so clear is what you can do for me when I am lying shackled in irons within those unholy walls, as you call them. But you are right, sir, I have no choice. My best chance lies with you, for I have little enough chance as it stands with people of the likes of Pharor and Peshkari." He grinned. "In addition to that, I am here and I do not really have much to do."

Ynnis broke into what looked like a relieved grin. "Count on me, Tanilorner," he said.

It was already growing dark as Thoric rode out of the palace. Just before sunset they had observed smoke rising from the temple garden, and all the gates were locked. Something was afoot, but even the King's spies were unable to report anything other than that strange preparations were being made and that no one was being allowed into the temple.

When the sun went down a silence fell over the city and also the jungle beyond the palisades, which caused great apprehension among the inhabitants who crept away furtively to lie low in their houses and huts.

The patrols of the watch reported that all the streets were empty, as though swept clean, and that an acrid smell from the smoke emanating from the palace garden hung heavy on the breeze.

Thoric rode cautiously along in the rapidly lengthening shadows of the houses. There were but few lamps alight, making the gloom all the more menacing.

Thoric reached the temple square unchallenged. A flicker of firelight crept over the high walls of the temple garden, illuminating the white-walled houses around it.

Suddenly a rushing noise rent the air. It came from all around, with a sound like the beating of wings, as though a mighty flock of large birds were fluttering over the city. Thoric stared up into the blackness of the night sky, but he could see nothing.

An icy blast blew across the square and the fluttering noise died away. Thoric shook his head. He had a feeling of no longer being alone, although he could not see anybody, and the square was bare. The temple gate formed a darker blotch in the darkness.

He dismounted, hesitantly. The King's assessment had obviously been incorrect. So much the better. The priests were busy with their own machinations, and the King had obviously overestimated the value they would place on the Tanilorner.

He shrugged his shoulders. Naturally, this meant his work was done. He could hardly go up and knock at the door, and say, "Here I am, do you not want me?"

He looked around him. Ynnis had described an inn which lay not far from the temple square, but he could see no welcoming light, and wandering about in the dark was not a prospect that filled him with rapture.

As he was about to mount his horse once more, a menacing sensation of danger came over him, stronger than he had ever felt before. A sudden pressure in his ears almost deafened him. He shook his head wildly, but the giddiness would not go away. Out of the corner of his eye he spied shapes scurrying away from the gates of the temple. He could not make them out very clearly, for they slipped from his half-blinded gaze before he could really see them. Nonetheless, he saw images, pale and half-formed, like visions in a dream, of winged beings with somber faces and glowing eyes.

Then the pressure went away, and his numbed senses cleared. Around him there was nothing but the night air, warm now, with nothing of the icy chill he remembered there had been before.

He shook his head again. Chilly winds and jumbled images? Did he have a fever? From somewhere in the night he thought he heard somebody cry out, but he did not know whether he could trust his ears. A moment later, however, all doubts about his senses vanished. The gate to the temple opened and a number of figures came scurrying out, running straight toward him.

It suddenly looked as though the King had been right. Thoric had to suppress a powerful urge to leap on his horse and gallop off. He took so long over it that they could not fail to catch him, but he did enough to make it seem as though he was trying to get away.

When they reached him they gave him no opportunity to dispute the outcome. Two leapt up at him, one tearing the reins from his grasp, while another aimed a blow at him, which missed. The whole incident took place completely soundlessly. Thoric's fighting spirit instinctively sprang into life. It was not in his nature simply to allow himself to be beaten into submission. He was used to defending himself, and old habits were not easily suppressed. For a while he succeeded in holding off all three of them. He reached for his dagger, only to realize that they had already wrenched it from his belt. So, they wanted him alive. So much the better. It was going to mean a bloody head for somebody!

Instantly they grabbed hold of him once more, and reinforcements had arrived in the interim. He fell to the ground under the sheer weight of numbers.

Oppressive silence was suddenly on him once more.

"Quickly!" roared one of the men. "They are coming. By all the gods!"

Thoric was not sure that he had understood the words correctly, but there was one thing that was unmistakable: the fear in Yshite's voice.

He was jerked to his feet, and received a heavy blow on the temple which knocked him unconscious before he could find out what it meant.

# 4

He could not have been unconscious for more than an instant, for when he awoke he could feel that he was still being carried. The men's gasps rang out with a hollow tone. They had to be in a hall—the great hall of the temple. Candlelight was all around him. The door closed with a creak. Somebody yelled out something, and there was more than a trace of panic in his voice.

Thoric tried to shake off his dizziness, but the dull ache in his head was not the only cause. It was as if the air were being compressed under a heavy weight, making breathing difficult.

Then the gate clanged shut, and the nightmare was over.

They put Thoric down and let him go, although they continued to watch him with a wary eye. Apart from the seven men who had brought him into the temple, all of whom were wearing the Gisha star on their helmets, there were a dozen priests in green robes embroidered with gold, standing before the altar which was illuminated by a great number of candles. The benumbing scent of honey and incense filled the hall. Another dozen figures stood on either side of the altar, younger men and youths in white cowls, temple servants and acolytes: The sorcerer was bent over the altar, his back turned to Thoric. Oil lamps hung from the ceiling, and shafts of light penetrated the smoky air.

The gigantic image of Aope stared menacingly through the smoke from behind the altar. The face of unearthly beauty was contorted into a cruel rictus. All eyes were turned toward the altar, and Thoric could not suppress the odd sensation that the goddess's face was somehow involved in what was happening—that it was filled with expectation—that the block of stone was alive, that a being was staring out through the emerald eyes.

The sorcerer spun round and contemplated Thoric. In his bony face shone a fanatical fire.

"A southerner," he said in fluent Wolsany. "His strength shall succeed where my imprecations seem to be failing. To the altar with him!"

The Gisha seized Thoric and dragged him forward. He struggled, but the seven of them succeeded in keeping him under control albeit with the greatest difficulty. A priest stepped forward and stopped them. He was an elderly man, with almost-white hair.

"Wait," he said turning to the sorcerer. "Not him . . . Master." It was obvious that the word came hard to him. There was something akin to loathing in his demeanor. "With this Tanilorner here we shall be able to force the King to release Pharor."

"You are an old fool, Iltar; and you underestimate the King. . . ."

"Perhaps he has plans of his own," the priest interrupted.

"You may depend on it. However, if I have interpreted the signs correctly, and if my spell succeeds, we shall be the only ones in E'lil able to make plans. We shall have an army that none will be able to withstand. But anyway, calm yourself—I do not want this southern barbarian's blood, merely his strength. Place him on the altar!"

The men lifted the fiercely struggling figure of Thoric and pushed him into the middle of the stone slab, without however releasing his arms. Upon a signal from the sorcerer, two acolytes brought up a dish and a silver jug. One of them poured out a quantity of a greenish liquid, and waited.

The sorcerer bent low over his victim's face, his bony features tense. Thoric felt as if the gaze of the wide-open eyes were boring into his head. Once more he felt that same pressure on his senses. He tried to tear himself away, but the men held him down with all their strength. Nor were their arms the only things that were hampering him: he was paralyzed by the Mythan's eyes. Their power had shortly so taken a grip on him that they held him as firmly as if he were shackled.

The wizard gave another signal. The men let the Tanilorner go. He lay there motionless. His fists were clenched, and his features screwed up in silent defiance, but not a muscle moved.

Thoric could see all that was going on around him, albeit that everything was slightly indistinct, as though seen through a veil—under this paralyzing spell he was nonetheless totally awake. When the sorcerer issued the order "Drink!" he opened his mouth just like some puppet.

The acolyte slowly emptied the dish into his

mouth. The greenish liquid had a bitter flavor, but this sensation was just as muted as those experienced by his eyes and ears.

After a while, a deep weariness came over him. He felt as if he were asleep. Then a dream came, and in it he could see clearly and distinctly, as though wide awake.

He was suddenly afraid.

The temple had vanished, and with it priests, acolytes, Gisha and even the sorcerer, although his voice came from close by, echoing in the void surrounding Thoric. He was speaking in a language of which Thoric understood even less than he did Yshite. The words were heavy with imploring and prayer.

Thoric ceased to pay any attention to the voice. The air surrounding him was chill. He was frozen to his very soul. The dark emptiness around him began to fill. Something came creeping slowly up on him, entering his senses. He had the disturbing feeling that whatever it was he was seeing had come from within himself, from inside his head. But that was impossible, for he had never before seen creatures such as these.

The things he was seeing were female—small, doll-like faces, bodies with the light bronze coloring of the races of Southern Wolsany. However, they were not so graceful, being tall and muscular like the firm-breasted women-warriors of Taphany.

Thoric was stricken with horror at the sight of the powerful feathered wings on which they swept through the black emptiness on their downward flight. They contemplated from behind eyes filled with the fires of Ether, with a diabolical temptation in their winsome features that presaged death. Some somber charm surrounded them, their movements, bodies, faces—and souls, if they possessed such a thing.

More and more of them came, settling in the black depths beneath him with gentle beatings of their great wings. For an instant he had the impression of hovering over a feebly glowing honeycomb, a regular lattice-work of hexagons that lay far below him. Like a living pillar, the winged women drifted down onto one of the tiny hexagons.

Somewhere in the back of his consciousness the sight of these hexagons stirred a vague memory. Bruss had spoken of hexagons. Frankari too. But he did not know what they meant.

Something to do with the Ether, or the Gods.

Then this impression and the memory paled and vanished, suddenly, as if somebody had been listening to his thoughts and had found them dangerous. Everything was extinguished from his consciousness, even the sight of the winged creatures.

Suddenly, he was filled with a desire to reach out and touch these female forms, but he was still unable to move. The throng of bodies around him grew even denser. Not once did he stop to wonder whence they came, nor why they were flying down into the black depths of the void.

Then, suddenly, they touched him. They reached out to him, in hungry caresses, with icy fingers. He felt as though death were upon him, their very touch draining all the life-force from him, and he was overcome with a sensation of weakness yet of ecstasy.

He yearned for their caresses, with a hunger no less compelling than that which their unearthly faces had engendered in him, and he pressed himself even harder into their cold hands.

Piercing the ghastly silence in which all this was

taking place, the imploring voice of the sorcerer still rang out loud and clear. This it was that jolted Thoric back to consciousness, and he became suddenly, horribly aware that he was dying. He began to resist them.

With every passing moment the longing and the surrender grew even fainter, as the sense of horror and defiance grew within him. Then he realized just how weak he already was, but panic conferred a strength on him which he never guessed that he had.

The nightmare image began to pale, slowly at first, but then more quickly, as he came to realize that he could break free of it.

All at once he was awake.

He was still in the temple. The sorcerer's face was screwed up in fury, and he looked exhausted. His hands were raised, as though he intended to strike Thoric. The breath made a rasping noise in his throat. Then he turned away.

Thoric felt a prickling sensation in his limbs. They were slowly waking from their paralysis. Priests were scurrying hither and thither about the great hall, in a state of great agitation. Thoric could not quite make out what was going on, but he noticed that the temple gates were open. Cries rang out in the hall, issuing from the throats of both men and women.

They were cries of mortal dread, of terror and despair.

Thoric's senses reeled. Nobody seemed to be concerned with him. The sorcerer's back was turned as he listened to events taking place outside the temple.

Thoric's faintness threatened to engulf him as he tried to stand up on the altar. Above him he saw

Aope's face of stone. Gilded pupils followed his every move, her features wearing an expression of diabolical lust, her mouth twisted into a malicious grin. But this was not aimed at Thoric—it was for the sorcerer—and he could not see it.

Thoric had the menacing feeling that something was afoot that none had ever experienced before—none but the owner of this face of stone, for there was no doubt in his mind that it was alive. Perhaps the sorcerer had conjured up more than he should have.

Thoric gathered all his strength, and although his legs threatened to give way under him he leapt to his feet. He landed, on his knees, at the sorcerer's side, and lashed out. The white-clad figure collapsed in a heap. The Tanilorner scrambled to his feet and staggered toward the open door. The priests paid him no attention. Nobody seemed to notice him but for the sorcerer, who was struggling to get to his feet—and the Goddess whose gaze followed Thoric's every movement. The expression in the eyes of gold caused the hairs to rise on the back of Thoric's neck. A chill hand clutching at his heart, Thoric reached the door and staggered out. He was no longer capable of logical thought. The idea of escape alone drove him on.

But the night city offered no shelter. It was itself a sacrificed offering in the nightmare from which Thoric had awakened, at least that was how it had seemed. But now it looked as though the horror was no dream, but reality.

The night sky was filled with shapes in flight, but now without that silence which had made everything seem so unreal. Eerie cries filled the air, cries of people suffering in their death throes and others, so unreal, as if of lost souls. The bodies however were that much more real. Not all of them were flitting about the night sky. There were great numbers of them hanging from the walls of houses, clawing at the shutters over the windows. Cries of terror rang out from inside the houses of those unfortunate souls whose shutters had not been fastened properly. Near the temple, a man dashed out into the street, closely pursued by two flying shapes striving to catch hold of him. He swung an axe, lashing out blindly around him. He cried out something that Thoric did not understand.

A moment later he was enveloped in a mass of fluttering bodies; he convulsed, turned over and then lay there motionless.

*Blood*! screamed Thoric's thoughts. *It is blood they want!* The victim's screams made it sound as if he were being overtaken by a terror which surpassed even death itself.

With a shudder, Thoric retreated to the temple gate. There was no escaping them. The flying creatures were swarming over the entire city like a huge flock of birds. There was no escaping them in the streets, and very few houses even were able to withstand the onslaught.

They had not yet espied him, but they would do so at any moment. Priests and acolytes were thronging around the gate, trying to catch a glimpse of the chaos. Their faces were white, their eyes wide with terror. They pulled the Tanilorner inside to safety and locked the gate.

Iltar's gaze was directed accusingly toward TrondasKhyn.

"When will it end?"

The sorcerer returned his gaze, fury in his face. "Do you not want power? Did you think you could attain it without . . .? You fools! The Powers of

Darkness are not something one can call up and similarly make disappear at will—they have their price. But they are weak. Never again will they be so cheap to buy as now, for their influence in this world grows less and less. It was with your agreement that I summoned them, now we shall use them together. I did not come all the way here from Kanzany to take heed of cowardice and the babblings of fools. I came here because nowhere else in all the continents of the world are the life-forces of the ancient gods still so strong, and Darkness so deeply rooted. This is now the only place where they may be conjured up and used. We have taken the first step. . . ."

"These creatures of Darkness of yours are slaughtering our people," said Iltar with an anger that he had the greatest difficulty in suppressing. "Is that their price? It is too high, Mythan. Perhaps human life means nothing to you since you are not yourself human."

"This Darkness of mine, did you say, worm?" hissed the sorcerer, drawing himself up threateningly to his full height before the priest. "It is also your Darkness. You it was who would conjure up the ancient gods, and were ready to make blood sacrifices as in olden times. This country has never been free of Darkness. It is within the hearts of men. There was a time when the whole of Ysh was one great temple of Darkness—not a glorious empire as your dreams of the past would have it, not a mighty people, but a pestilential boil on the face of the world, an empire of slaves." He laughed mockingly at the expressions of confusion on the faces of the priests. "And *we* . . . mark it well, priest! . . . *we* put an end to that. We were never the slaves of Darkness, only ever its masters!"

"This time, however, it will be different!" The voice was a mere whisper, coming from somewhere within the room. The sorcerer gave a start. The priests looked around them, white-faced.

Thoric stared up into the face of the Goddess. It terrified him. There was a mocking smile on the face. The strong mouth did not move as the voice issued forth, but Thoric was certain that it was the Goddess speaking.

"My priestess has altered the balance of the world. Darkness has been beaten back, and Life will triumph—for a while. Your army, Mythan, will prove to be a mere illusion, for Darkness will carry all before it. I too shall march, for I am born of you. My temple is one of the last gates left. It will be open to all creatures that are not creatures of Life."

Then silence.

Iltar was the first to regain his power of speech. "The Goddess has spoken to us—we must pay heed to what she says."

"Your words no longer have any meaning," the sorcerer interrupted. "Aope is to disappear, just like everything else born of Darkness, and all that is connected with it."

"And your own powers, TrondasKhyn? Nothing will remain of the Mythanen powers, is that not true?" sneered one of the preists.

"Enough to annihilate people such as you," replied the wizard coldly. "Mark well one thing, priest. For the mighty in spirit there will always be a bridge across to the Powers of the Ether. Here! Look closely, and then scoff, if you will!"

He raised his hands high above his head. The wide arms of the cowl began to flap and flutter. For a moment he stood there as though spellbound, his features testifying to the vast power of his will.

Then his hands began slowly to move, beckoning, enticing, half crooked like claws. The gigantic statue of Aope began to move! First it raised an arm, then a foot, advancing with a sound of crunching stone. Then there came a dull thud against the door, followed by a second, and a third.

Everybody gave a startled cry, sorcerer, priests and acolytes alike. Thoric spun round, feeling a clammy hand clutching at his heart. He could visualize what was happening outside. The creatures of Darkness were seeking out the door that led back to their own realm. The temple was that door, Aope had said.

Another crunching sound caused the men to back away hurriedly. The sorcerer stared up with frightened eyes at the statue. It seemed to have slipped from his control, and was continuing to advance. The powerful arm came down and smashed the altar to pieces. The priests retreated still farther. The raised foot came down and crushed the debris to a powder.

The sorcerer began to run. The fear dormant in all sorcerers had come alive in him—the fear that the spirits which he conjured up might, just once, prove stronger than he. He had underestimated this particular adversary. He ran for the door, never once turning back to look at his pursuer. He did not therefore see that the stone into which he had caused life to return was stiff once more, that Aope no longer obeyed him. Only its impetus had caused the colossus to continue its advance.

The sorcerer wrenched the door open before the priests could stop him. He stood there confronted by a wall of dark bodies, with gleaming, intoxicated eyes. He let out a shriek and reeled backwards. One of the priests tried to close the door, but it was too late.

Like a great wave the winged creatures of Darkness came flooding in. The wizard fell to the floor under the weight of the assault. A scream filled the temple. The beating of hundreds of pairs of wings turned the air inside the temple into a whirlwind.

Thoric watched them streaming to the altar and flying upwards, like a great living pillar right up into the dome.

With a thunderous crack the roof burst asunder. Masonry rained down, crushing priests and acolytes. Those creatures that fell mutilated and injured to the floor under the hail of stonework tried to fly up there once more, and were caught in the round-dance of wings beating. No blood flowed from their wounds, no cries of pain escaped from their icy lips. There was no life in them—merely a terrifying power which gave the appearance of life to the substance of their bodies.

Close to Thoric, great chunks of wall were coming away, covering everything in dust and fragments of stone, with sounds like claps of thunder, in chaos. He tottered and fell to the floor. Before losing consciousness, he felt a searing pain in his arms and legs, as if teeth were being sunk into his flesh, although it might only have been sharp splinters of stone.

# 5

A familiar face was bending over Thoric.

"Ynnis," he croaked in relief.

The Yshite smiled. "I said I would come to fetch you."

Thoric nodded. "Yes, you did say that." He looked around him. He was lying in a small room, bare but for a bed and a trunk. "Where am I?"

"Still in the temple, Tanilorner."

Thoric lifted himself up on his elbows. "In the temple?"

"Or rather, in what is left of it, my friend. Fear not, much has changed this night."

"So, it was not all a nightmare," muttered Thoric.

"No," declared Ynnis in a depressed tone of voice. "The city stinks of death. Men, women and children—all were sacrificed equally. The huts look as though a hurricane had swept through them. Only the very strongest houses were able to withstand the onslaught of those creatures. They even managed to get into the west wing of the palace.

We fought against them with swords—it was futile. Two dozen of my best men died before we discovered that fire would drive them away. Then it became easier, although it was still hell. . . ."

"Where is the sorcerer?" asked Thoric, biting back the pain in his limbs caused by sitting up and swinging his legs from the bed. Ynnis shook his head. "Nobody knows. It would appear that the creatures took him with them, although the priests rather doubt that."

"Who brought me here? You?"

Ynnis shook his head. "No. Iltar. He was one of the few to survive the destruction of the temple. But you should not try to get up. Some of the palace guard are on their way here. They will take you to my quarters, and the King's physician will attend to your wounds."

"That will not be necessary," said a voice from the doorway. The aged, friendly face of Iltar was looking at them, serious of mien. "Rise gently, Thoric of Chara. You are simply a little weak, and the food of the palace will help you with that." He gave a tired smile, and Thoric noticed that he had one foot heavily bandaged, and was limping. As for his own body, he saw a number of wounds on his arms and legs. They were not bandaged, but they had been smeared with a greenish ointment, which formed a brittle shield.

It hurt him to move, but nothing seemed to have been broken. He grinned—and could almost have screamed in agony. It felt as though his chin and part of the back of his head were missing.

"Are you sure that he is able to stand?" asked Ynnis.

"That is another matter," replied the priest with a smile. "But the sooner he tries the better."

Thoric sat up, but immediately sank back onto the bed with a sigh. His knees felt as weak as cream cheese.

"Where is the sorcerer?" he asked the priest.

The latter shook his head. "Nobody saw him ride away, but that does not necessarily mean anything. These Mythanen have other means of making their getaway. He could not have come from where he did by natural methods. The highlands of Kanzany are under heavy falls of snow. There is no way through, either on horseback or by sled. So how he got here . . ." Iltar shrugged his shoulders.

"What did it all mean?" asked Thoric. "What really happened? I mean where did they come from, those . . . those . . . beings . . .?"

"ThrondasKhyn conjured them up."

"Where did they come from, the Ether?"

"Many of the peoples of Magira have ancient legends about an eternal battle fought between the powers of Darkness and the powers of Life, symbolizing the eternal battle between good and evil which goes on inside every man. But there are signs to show that these legends are . . . not merely legends. . . ."

"The Rider of Darkness," murmured Thoric. "I have seen him."

The priest nodded. "He is one of those signs. Too many have seen him for him to be merely a phantom. Some of the priests have discovered scriptures and prayers in the pyramids, to Gods who are themselves legends . . . bloody, cruel Gods to whom our people once prayed and brought blood sacrifices. Dreams of former glory blinded them, Peshkari above all. They believed that if they were to build new altars to these ancient Gods then the glories of yesteryear would also return. They were like children. They misinterpreted the signs. They forgot the realities of their dreams."

"Would they have succeeded then?"

"To a certain extent, yes. But not now. It would seem that Life is stronger than Darkness. Aope would no longer respond, and the Messengers of Darkness returned to their own realm. The seers will interpret the omens once more. Perhaps we are now freer of the past than previously. The future belongs to the barbarians, as much to the overlords of Wolsany as to those from the North."

"Does that mean that your people's religion is dead?"

"No, our religion is not dead, but the Goddess of the eternal forest will no longer hear, no longer respond. She is no more than a stone idol, just like the gods of the barbarians."

"Is Ilara free then?" exclaimed Thoric.

"Ilara . . .?" Iltar shook his head. "The priestess is closer to Aope than any of us. She will not come back, Tanilorner. She carries the seed of Darkness within her."

"The seed of Darkness?" asked Thoric in blank incomprehension. "What does that mean?"

He shrugged. "Those were the sorcerer's words. They may have much significance, or none at all."

"The sorcerer said that? Where did he find out about . . .?"

"It was one of his breed that made off with her in Vanada. What is known to one of them is known to all of them. That is the secret of their wisdom."

"Then he also knows what happened to her!"

"Perhaps, although it seems incredible that they could know what goes on beyond the Ether. If they had known that they would long ago have become masters of the world."

"Did you say that he comes from Kanzany?"

Iltar nodded slowly.

"Whereabouts?"

"From the highlands of Arullu, so I have heard. He is perhaps a counselor of the King, or a sage to one of the many princes. If you wish to find him you have a hard road ahead of you. Do not attempt it before the end of winter. Merchants are always the first to chance it, for profit. They take many risks, but not even they would take the one of trying it in winter. . . ."

Thoric sat up once more, and this time he stood up too. He overcame his feeling of weakness. He reached his hand out to Iltar and shook the priest's hand heartily.

"I have to thank you, priest. I do not know if I am happy at the course events have taken . . . but, in any case, thank you."

The city looked like a gigantic charnel-house. Great funeral pyres were stacked up in front of the gates. The warmish breezes were already wafting the stench of putrefaction across the ruins of the huts. Inside the cool stone and marble houses it was a little better. Vultures circled in great flocks over the roofs.

To remain in this city where there would shortly be so much pestilence held little attraction for Thoric. But there was Ynnis' hospitality which he could hardly refuse, all the more so in that his departure for Kanzany was far from imminent.

It would not be his first journey there. He had spent more than a year in Movus when he was a corsair plying up and down the coasts of the Endless Ocean. He knew well enough the people, language and customs. The prospect of going back to Kanzany delighted him.

He still lived in hopes that Thuon had set out on his trail and was on his way to E'lil. It was another reason to wait a while longer. But every day the chances of this became more and more slight, and finally he ceased to cherish the hope altogether.

Their adventure which had begun so well had not had a good ending with Bruss and Ilara gone and likewise Frankari, the strange foreigner. And what about Thuon, with whom he had been hoping to make the journey north?

It was unlikely that their paths would cross again.

It was better to rid oneself of old memories. If war was imminent, as everybody thought, then the north was a surer place for a free spirit and adventurer such as he.

The North attracted him.

And so one day he joined a caravan taking goods to the coast. The winter rains had set in in the meantime and storms made crossing Hero Straits a hazardous undertaking. When they finally abated, the omens of war were even more obvious. Wolsany warships were sailing up and down the coasts of Ysh.

The old priest had been right. The ancient traditions were doomed to disappear. New ones had to be created.

And bloody war made the best historians.

*At this point, Thoric is already in the distant East. No longer does he see any signs of Wolsany fleets gathering in Hero Straits. Storms drive the merchant's ship, the merchant whose caravan he has joined, far out into the Endless Ocean.*

*At the beginning of the month of the Wolf,*

*the last month of winter, they eventually see the coast of Kanzany ahead of them. They reach Movus, one of the few safe harbors in these rough waters.*

*He does not stay long in the port, although he is warned against riding into the highlands. With two old acquaintances who finally get talked into acting as his guides, he eventually leaves for Lobotan, and from there they take a caravan route up into the mountains.*

# 6

The market-place of Sambun proved to be a widely-scattered collection of wooden stalls under whose multicolored, fluttering awnings farmers artisans, merchants and swordsmiths offered their wares for sale in total harmony while forever keeping a watchful eye on the gaily-colored crowd in which there lurked the common enemy: the light-fingered thief. It was not rare to hear the shrill cry of "Sassan!" as the people of Kanzany called thieves. Sassan—the devil of the airs, the omnipresent who could disappear into thin air. Most of the time, at least.

The man standing in the shadows of the entrance to a narrow alleyway surveyed the sunlit square with eyes screwed up to lessen the glare. He was tall and blond, in striking contrast with the dark-haired and generally smallish local people hurrying about their business. His sun-bronzed skin also differed from that of the Kanzany. However, what stood out the most was his clothing, so different from the long multicolored shirts and the trousers of heavy material which the people up here in the highlands wore under their thick sheepskin coats. Under his own half-open coat, made of white polar-bear fur, there gleamed a breast-plate and from his broad leather belt there hung a dagger and the empty sheath of a short Wolsany sword. His trousers too were of white fur, and they disappeared into a pair of high boots. His head was bare, and his yellow hair fluttered in the cold wind of the month of the Wolf.

Winter still reigned up in the highlands of Arullu, but the sun was now just beginning to reach out with its powerful hands toward the ice and snow, thawing the white covering in the streets, and the spirits of the inhabitants which had been locked away for winter. The curious glances they cast at the foreigner were not unfriendly. He was the harbinger of coming spring, the first to venture over the snowbound passes over which the merchants' caravans would shortly follow.

The man's face was hard, and seemed to convey a sense of coldness to the casual observer. But when he smiled, his eyes laughed too, giving his stubborn features an air of open geniality.

For a while the stranger stood and watched the hurly-burly of the market, and then he stopped one of the market-goers hurrying past.

"I have been told that there is a good swordsmith here. Where might I find him?"

"Indeed there is, stranger. He is to be found at the far end of the square. You will hear the smithy from some way away."

The foreigner nodded his thanks, and made his way through the dense throng into a narrow street between the stalls. He found the bumping and jostling of the people quite pleasant after the loneliness of the Kanzany mountains, but nonetheless he kept his hands firmly pressed to his dagger and his money pouch. Very shortly he heard the sound of hammer on metal. He cast scarcely a look at any of the stalls around him. There was nothing that attracted him—principally because the gold in his pouch was set aside for the sword, which he needed more than anything. He had thought of little else during the long journey from the coast.

The forge was a little low building made of stone, and there was hardly any snow on the roof. A violent hissing sound came from inside, and a cloud of dirty gray steam shot out of a hole in the roof. The man held his breath and stepped inside. He had the hollow feeling that his polar-bear skin was about to lose its whiteness.

His eyes took a long while to get used to the dark. Steam was still rising from a stone sink. The master blacksmith was standing by the fire, holding a blade in the glowing coals while an assistant fanned the flames. Their faces were blackened with the smoke. The stranger drew his cloak more tightly round him.

The swordsmith's apprentice looked up. He nodded to his master who turned round.

"I should like to buy a sword," said the stranger.

The swordsmith gave him a searching look. Finally he nodded.

"You look as if you know how to use one."

He strode out of the smithy, leaving the stranger either to follow him or wait where he was. Slightly confused he followed him into the house next door. He was in such a hurry that he failed to notice the Kanzany merchant who was studying him pensively. After a moment's indecision, the merchant too walked into the house.

Inside a small room, the stranger's gaze was treated to a collection of swords, lances, axes and spears, which he spent a long time examining minutely. At last he whirled round to the expectant swordsmith, and in a tone of evident ill-humor, declared, "All these swords are curved!"

"Just like the paths trodden by the gods!" replied the swordsmith. He picked up one of the swords and brandished it about in the air, with a little whistling noise. As he did so, he moved his rather ungainly body in an agile manner. There was a glint in his eye.

The stranger made a dismissive gesture with his hand. "What do I care about the paths trodden by the gods? I need a good sword for wherever my own path takes me. I know of your people's holy dances, and the significance of that knife, but my intentions include no dancing about along this coast. Give me a sword that cuts a good swathe, and lunges well."

The swordsmith stared at him in bewilderment.

"Dancing . . . knife . . .!" he whispered. Then he spun round abruptly. "Watch this!" He pointed to a crude wooden doll dressed in the chain-mail shirt of the army of the Kanzany falcon and a light helmet. A dark line could be seen across its throat. "Mark it well, stranger!"

Letting out the battle cry of the falcon, the swordsmith leapt up in front of the doll, raised the curved sword in the air and with lightning speed dragged it across the doll's throat. With a scraping noise the sharp cutting edge slashed through the wood, exactly along the dark line. It sank right in, as if into a lump of soft clay.

The doll's head fell back.

The stranger nodded, unimpressed. "Not a bad bit of dancing. But put an axe or a sword in his hand, and give him strength and agility, and teach him the art of swordplay." He looked at the doll contemptuously. "A good lunge is worth more than a dozen of your slashes."

"Never!' cried the swordsmith. "Nothing separates body from soul so well as a curved blade, as it slices the head off in one blow. Pierce the heart and the soul still lives in the body. But sever the head from the trunk and death is then total."

"Death is death," retorted the stranger, who loathed the barbaric custom of decapitation, still encountered so often in this country. Nothing held such sway over these people of the east as fear of the dead. "We have a saying in my country:

'A sword with curve no good can serve!' "

"Bah, sayings!" retorted the swordsmith furiously.

"I have often found it to be justified," the stranger continued calmly. "I was riding out from Lobotan with two friends. We had just reached the mountains when a horde of brigands fell upon us, like snow-devils incarnate. . . ."

"And?"

"They are dead!" replied the stranger. "They still have their heads, but they are dead all right!"

"Southerner, you are a fool." A smile of triumph played on the swordsmith's lips, with a flash of white teeth. "Did you not say that you had two friends? What has happened to them? Did you go your separate ways?"

"They too are dead."

"Which goes to show . . ." the swordsmith began.

"Which goes to show something other than what you think," the foreigner interrupted. "They were of your people, and they died with a curved sword in their hand. And now, swordsmith, cease trying to convert me. Give me a straight blade which will come alive in my hand and will not crack when it hits something hard, and you shall receive your payment in the finest gold."

"You will be unlucky," said a voice, causing both of them to look up in surprise.

In the doorway stood a man of middle age, dressed in rich clothing. His features bore the distinctive stamp of the Orient. However he differed noticeably from the inhabitants of Sambun. His skin had none of the yellow pigmentation of the people of Kanzany, and on his chin he sported a black beard, as long as a man's finger, and growing up his cheeks. A round hat of the same brown color as his coat covered his dark hair. His eyes were lively. In his hand he carried a cane, and he pointed to the swordsmith with it.

"He can only make what he knows—what his father made, and his father before that—the crescent of the waning moon. For these people the crescent is the essence of everything." He smiled.

"Ah, Micolai," cried the swordsmith. "The heads of barbarians are filled with rubbish. You know about far-off lands. Are they all like this?"

"He comes from the south," Micolai explained. "There they build roads as straight as their swords, and they measure glory by the rays of the sun. Their women are as slender as their swords. The only curve they like is that of the heavens, and the endless horizon. People are different, my friend, as are their needs. I have that which you seek, foreigner."

"Are you a merchant?" asked the stranger.

Micolai nodded once more.

"Good," said the foreigner, relieved, "I shall buy it."

Micolai gave a sign of refusal. "Leave your pouch where it is. It is you that I need, Thoric of Chara. . . ."

The stranger raised his eyebrows. "How do you know my name?"

Micolai shrugged. "You are staying at SasKan's house. He knows your name, and once one person in this town knows something, then it does not remain a secret for very long."

Thoric shook his head. "Curved swords and loose tongues," he muttered.

The swordsmith grinned and replaced the doll's head.

"Take him with you, Micolai. I have had enough of this barbarian's prattling."

Thoric spun round angrily, but when he saw the laughter in the swordsmith's eyes he too broke into a grin. He clapped the merchant on the shoulder so fiercely that the latter winced in pain, despite the padding of his heavy cloak. "That is the way I feel too. Come, let us go. I saw a tavern not far from here, and if there is one thing about this country that I do like, it is the wine. In great curved barrels!" His laugh echoed round the forge.

The small room in the tavern was almost empty when they entered. Thoric turned his nose up. The sweetish smell of opium pipes came from closed adjoining rooms. The proprietor was a plump Kanzany, with tiny eyes almost totally hidden under heavy lids. In the feeble flickering light from the few scant candles, however, he had a friendly look about him and was otherwise quite quick-witted, a quality which Thoric had learned to prize in these industrious people with the crescent-shaped soul. A moment later, pewter tankards of fiery sparkling red wine stood on the table in front of them. Thoric raised his in a toast.

"To the dead, merchant!" he cried.

"Aye, and that they stay dead," the latter rejoined.

They drank, and the innkeeper instantly came rushing over to refill their tankards.

Thoric looked at him in obvious displeasure. "Do you not have a jug?"

The proprietor stared at him in bewilderment. "A jug, for wine?"

"Where I come from we serve wine on the table in jugs, and the customer pours it out for himself."

"We keep only oil and flour in jugs, Sir," the innkeeper stammered, his thoughts rather muddled. "Wine would go off in jugs. . . ."

"It would if you gave it time to do so," retorted Thoric.

Micolai turned round smiling. "I fear that people around here do not have such dry throats as you southerners. Bring us some fresh wine."

The landlord hurried to collect their tankards and fill them from the barrel; he set them back down on the table. Thoric waited until he had walked away again.

"About this sword then?"

"I have several—you may take your pick," stated the merchant. "But I need your help. The sword shall be your reward. Plus a pouch of gold—and a girl's smile."

"Only a smile?" Thoric laughed at the embarrassment on the face of the man sitting opposite him. "Please excuse the coarse joke, my friend. Who is this girl?"

"My daughter. She is aged sixteen summers. Because at thirteen she was already of extraordinary beauty, Prince HalJin selected her . . ."

"For what purpose?"

Micolai sighed. "There is in this country an ancient law whereby the Prince has the right to the first night with any girl. When our people came here three hundred years ago, we united all the widely scattered tribes of Kanzany into one empire. We governed them and taught them our crafts and they taught us theirs, to the extent that the cry of the falcon is now on the lips of us both. We were few in number, or so our forefathers said. Many of the ancient customs of the local tribes rubbed off on us. . . ."

"Tell me," Thoric interrupted, "in a city such as this a Prince has in reality little time for government. Indeed, I saw so many girls in the market that I must grant you people of Kanzany one thing. Despite all the curved and crooked things here, and following on from your words: you must have very fit princes!"

Micolai smiled. "The custom does not make it a prince's duty, merely a right! Which means quite simply that he takes his pick, no more no less. And beauty is not always the deciding factor. The reasons are . . . manifold." His smile broadened. "It is a great honor, and it entails a certain obligation toward the Prince's court—and there always exists the possibility that the first-born will be of royal blood. The only condition is that the girl must appear before the Prince in all virginal purity. If she does not, ignominy and curses will accompany her forever more." Micolai sighed once more, heavier this time. "Not only her, but her family as well."

Thoric nodded silently. He began to understand. The little one had not been able to wait. But what could he do about it?

Micolai noticed his questioning glance, and went on rapidly: "She was chosen because she was beautiful. She still is," he added hastily, watching the Southerner closely to gauge the effect of his words. "She did not know that she was chosen. I thought she would be . . . I thought she was. . ." he broke off in confusion when he saw that Thoric was striving with all his might to suppress a grin.

Furious, he explained, "I discovered it on the last evening, when they came to fetch her to take her to the palace. Thoric!" He grasped the latter's arm. "In two days' time it will be the feast of the sun, and then she is to share the Prince's bed. We do not have much time." His voice trembled. "If he finds out that she . . ." he broke off meaningfully.

"Then what?" Thoric asked.

"We shall all be taken to the pillory," said Micolai in a broken voice. "Do you know what that means? Have you ever seen a pillory?"

"Yes, in the harbor at Movus. They had a thief there." The Southerner gave a shiver. "You really do have strange laws. It is only right and just that you too should suffer that fate."

The merchant heaved a sigh. "The swordsmith was right. You speak with all the coarseness of the barbarian. But you should know this—it is not for my own sake that I seek your help. As of this evening I shall no longer be in Sambun. Think of the girl. Do it for her sake."

"I shall do it for the sword," said Thoric, unmoved.

"Good, good," conceded Micolai. "For the sword then." He drank, nervously. These barbarians were damned difficult to handle.

"What do you wish of me?"

"You must free SiShin,"explained the Kanzany.

"SiShin?"

"My daughter."

"From the palace?"

Micolai nodded.

Thoric laughed softly. "Only a merchant could come up with such a stupid suggestion!"

"You are strong, you are daring. You are the only one in this city who would try it," said the Kanzany urgently. "Your arrival in the city I interpreted as a sign from the gods. . . ."

"What makes you think that I could be foolish enough to take on such a hazardous venture?" growled Thoric.

"You are an adventurer," replied the merchant. "All adventurers act like fools at times. I am sure," he added seeing that Thoric was about to speak, "that you have before now risked your life for less than a sword and a pouch of gold."

"That is true!" admitted the southerner pensively.

He drummed his fingers on the table. The landlord came rushing over eagerly. Micolai waved him away energetically.

"Is there some way of getting into the palace unseen?"

"Certainly," Micolai assured him.

"Do you know where the girl is?"

The Kanzany bit his lip. "I am not sure, but all the women are to be found in the white tower. There is no good reason why she should not be there."

Thoric rose to his feet. "Verify that before darkness falls, and find out about guards. . . ."

"But . . . how . . . ?" Micolai interrupted.

"That, merchant, is your problem. You will find me at SasKan's house. . . ." When he reached the door, he turned once more to the dumbfounded Kanzany. "And do not forget the sword!"

# 7

The whole day long Thoric wandered about in the vicinity of the palace. He talked to soldiers and farmers, beggars and thieves, and at one of the numerous fountains where they had smashed a hole through the ice he met a girl who had herself once been inside the palace. When he returned to Sas-Kan's house that evening, he had learned a lot—including the fact that it was almost impossible to get into Prince HalJin's palace. Or to get out again alive if one had not been invited in in the first place. For a time he toyed with the idea of seeking an audience in order to get inside the palace. Foreigners were rarely unwelcome visitors to the courts of princes because they had many tales to tell, and they thus brought variety into the monotony of a city cut off for the winter. But then everybody's attention would be on him, and he would have little opportunity to slip away and free the girl. No, it would not be very wise to follow that course of action. But then the only other possibility was even less wise. He smiled to himself at the thought of how often in his life he had given a single thought to the wisdom of his deeds. Nonetheless, the idea of seeking an audience still floated round in his head for a while afterwards. It was only when the merchant arrived that he finally dismissed it completely. Besides which, it might already be too late if the Prince were to refuse to see him.

The Kanzany was pale with excitement. "I have news," he whispered, casting a cautious look up and down the hall before closing the door. He placed a dark leather bag on the floor in front of Thoric, the contents of which made a gentle grating noise.

"Can anybody hear us here?"

Thoric grinned and shook his head.

"Well, SiShin is in the chamber at the very top of the white tower."

Thoric nodded in agreement. "I found that out too."

"The guards also sleep in the tower. One has to go through the guardroom to get into the tower. . . ."

Thoric's grin became broader. "They do more than just sleep there, I presume?"

But Micolai was too filled with enthusiasm to notice the tone of mockery in the Southerner's voice. "No, they are awake, of course, and the guard is changed at sunrise and sunset. There are a dozen women and girls in the tower. One of them is the Prince's sister, TayaSar, and another is his daughter TanaSai, the apple of his eye. The guards watch her jealously. One is his wife, Princess ValYa, and it is commonly rumored in the city that she is possessed by a demon which is awakened by the sight of blood."

Micolai cast him a doubtful glance. "There are many rumors in the city. The others are maids, simple servants and handmaidens, who attend to the well-being of the noble ladies. Only the Prince and a few trusted friends have entry to the tower, but I have not been able to discover who these trusted friends are. One of them, however, is certain to be ChuenGoch, Commander of the Prince's bodyguard. You must be wary of him. He is strange, uncanny."

"How does one get to the tower?"

"To get to it unseen you have to go through the garden. It is one part of the palace buildings that is swarming day and night with soldiers and guards. Even the garden is not without sentries, but not much light gets through the bushes. You will not be able easily to cover your tracks in the snow, but the darkness will help you. . . ."

"Us," Thoric corrected him. "It will help *us*, because you are to accompany me!"

Micolai's eyes widened. "But . . . but . . ." he stammered. His face became ashen when Thoric dismissed his protest.

"But me no buts. I have seen the palace for myself. The only way to get inside is through one of the three gates. We must snuff out two guard posts. That will not be difficult. But an unguarded gate will be noticed very quickly. Therefore you will put on a sentry's clothing and stay at the gate. . . ."

"I shall die of fear," groaned Micolai.

"Many have thought that," said Thoric unsympathetically, "but few have actually done so." He hesitated. "There is one other thing that I must know. Is there a sorcerer at the Prince's court?"

"Yes," stammered Micolai, "but he is not always here. He comes and goes as he sees fit. It is, however, rumored that the Prince owes him a great deal."

"What is his name?"

The merchant shook his head regretfully. "No one knows."

"Have you ever heard the name TrondasKhyn?"

Micolai shook his head. "I should certainly have remembered it if I had; it is an unusual name."

Thoric fell into a pensive silence. Perhaps he was on the right track, and perhaps not. Had not the aged Yshite priest said that what was known to one of them was known to them all? If so, then it might not be so important to find TrondasKhyn, and he might in fact learn more from a sorcerer who did not know his face.

"Have you brought the sword with you?" he asked Micolai abruptly.

The merchant pointed with trembling hand toward the large leather bag. Thoric undid it and pulled out the blade. "Ah!" he exclaimed appreciatively. His eyes lit up as his gaze wandered lovingly across the shining metal, the gilded handle, the slightly curved hand-guard, the strange talismanic shapes and figures that sparkled up at him from the gleaming blade. It was longer than the Wolsany sword he had worn before, and heavier. Nonetheless, it seemed to offer the same response to the hand that wielded it.

"Where did you come by such a sword?" he asked breathlessly.

"From a northerner named Aesor. I met him by the Sea of Heaven. . . ."

"Sea of Heaven?"

"It is a great lake to the West, right on the border of our country," explained Micolai, still horror-stricken. "I have heard people say that the Assu flows into the sea, but none has ever seen the mouth of the Assu. . . ."

"I have heard of it," murmured Thoric. "And of savage warlike hordes pressing ever farther south—and no wonder," he stroked the cold metal gently, "with swords like this! And yet it is long and heavy. That means one has to be strong just to overcome its inertia. For that one has to have arms as strong as a bear's. . . ."

"They have them," the Kanzany interrupted. "They are tall and savage, and their hair is as if on fire. They carry great round shields. But they also fight among themselves, when they throw their shields away, and take up these swords with both hands. Their movements seem completely devoid of inertia. They are as agile as if the wings on their helmets were wings on their bodies. . . ." He looked at Thoric with eyes that pleaded for mercy. "Do you really want to take me with you?"

"Certainly!"

"It is a dangerous plan. I shall be trembling with fear—it will betray us instantly. . . ."

"It will be dark," retorted Thoric, unmoved. "Nobody will see you trembling."

"But they will hear it. The sentry's mail-shirt . . . it will rattle like a sack full of gold coins . . . it will bring people round me . . . soldiers, thieves . . . and murderers. . . !"

"Then you will not get bored!"

"But one of them is sure to recognize me!" wailed Micolai.

"Good! They will be so occupied with you that I shall be able to get on with freeing the girl in peace," said Thoric with a laugh.

"What a hard heart beats within your barbarian breast," lamented the merchant, already in his mind incarcerated in the Prince's torture chamber, which is where he was sure he would end up.

Thoric rummaged about in the leather bag, and fetched out a tightly corked metal flask. "What is this?"

Micolai came dashing over to him when he saw that the southerner was about to open it. "Careful! It is poison!"

"Poison?" exclaimed Thoric. He raised the flask high above his head, and the Kanzany's crooked fingers clawed at thin air. "What is this for, serpent?"

"Fool! Leave it alone!" croaked Micolai.

"Very well, little shopkeeper. What is it for?"

"We shall need it this night. It sends people fast asleep just as soon as it enters their bloodstream."

"My sword does much the same thing, so why do we need this?"

"Because those that come into contact with your sword do not get up again," cried Micolai urgently.

"Yes, that could be so," mused Thoric.

"But this is simpler, much simpler! Let me explain."

Thoric pushed the clamoring Kanzany away from him.

"Very well, but not if you keep trying to talk with your arms and legs!"

"Good, good." The Kanzany dropped his arms.

"I can do nothing against brute force." He sank back onto the bed, raging. "Listen, you strength-lover. I came by this liquid many years ago from a sorcerer in Upzabab. I have never used it, but I have guarded it as I would a precious treasure. He swore by the sacred gods that he who drank of this potion, or who should get some in a cut or scratch would instantly sink into a deep sleep lasting two days and two nights. He told me to dip a dagger in it. That is what we are now going to do . . ."

"Many years ago, you say?" Thoric cast him a dubious glance. "Who is to say whether the spell will still work?"

"That will be evident if we try it out," continued Micolai eagerly.

Thoric nodded hesitantly. "But be warned, shopkeeper. Should it just occur to you to fall asleep before we reach the gate I shall throw you to the guards, asleep though you be!"

"Do you not trust me?" exclaimed the Kanzany.

"No," declared Thoric, breaking into a grin at the sight of Micolai's pitiful mien. Very slowly, he handed the flask back, grinning all the more as the Kanzany tore it angrily from his grasp.

"Your dagger, barbarian!"

With a laugh Thoric passed the shopkeeper his dagger. He looked on with interest as the Kanzany opened the metal flask, setting the cork carefully down on the ground. He sniffed at the open bottle.

"It is odorless," he proclaimed.

Then he held the blade out flat in front of him, raised the flask, and tilted it carefully. A drop of dark blue liquid appeared at the neck of the flask and fell onto the shiny metal of the knife splattering just a little. It hardened instantly to a tough, dark patina.

"It is certain still to retain its magical power," whispered Micolai agitatedly. He made to grasp the cutting edge, but Thoric knocked the blade aside.

"No tricks!"

Micolai cast the Southerner a reproachful look, but said nothing. He began to pour the liquid over the whole blade. It was a difficult proposition, and several times the two men had to leap smartly out of the way as drops fell to the floor, spraying items in the vicinity with a cloud of fine droplets. It was done. The dagger shimmered with a dark blue sheen in the flickering candlelight.

Thoric took it carefully in his hand and examined it suspiciously. He took the sword and scraped it across the surface of the dagger. Only by pressing with all his might did he succeed even in scratching it, but he could not remove any of it. He dragged the cutting edge across the surface of the table. The dagger bit deeply into it. It had obviously lost none of its keenness. Finally the Southerner broke into a grin. Micolai watched him expectantly.

"I have come to learn not to rely on amulets and other instruments of magic, but I do value them as occasional surprise aids. Here, do the same to the sword as well." He handed the blade to the much-relieved Kanzany. "How long will the treatment last?"

Micolai shrugged. "Only the gods know that, and even then not precisely."

Thoric laughed. "That is the right attitude. But now you must hurry—this is the darkest hour of the night and your compatriots are at their most fearful."

# 8

The streets were deserted, and only the faint glow of the stars was to be seen. The snow crunched under the feet of the two men as they hurried to the palace, a blazing oasis of light amid the darkness.

It was cold, and the men's breath gave off steam like the fiery breath of a hazzonish dragon in the air stiff with frost. Rare were the low stone houses where lights still shone; most of the doors and windows were barricaded with wooden shutters. Even the taverns were locked and dark, and Thoric had the odd sensation that the night belonged exclusively to the Prince and his courtiers. They crossed the marketplace with its empty stalls, and then Moon Square with its mighty mute temples and ornaments glistening with ice.

Thoric gathered his polar-bear skin more tightly around him. The cold took his breath away. The Kanzany stumbled along doggedly behind him, fingers clasped tightly around the handle of the dagger—and not merely because of the cold.

A black shadow detached itself from the darkness of a house, followed by two others—they came rushing at the two night-strollers. Micolai let out a shriek of terror and raised his dagger in defense. His attacker recoiled with a yell, his knife falling to the ground as he clapped his hands to his masked face. At the same moment Thoric ran the second assailant through with his sword. The man's cry was short and shrill. Both attackers sank into the snow without a sound. The third beat a hasty retreat and disappeared into the night, cursing.

"Yes, oh yes, nights in Sambun," growled Thoric, bending over to get a closer look at his would-be murderer. In the darkness, however, he could be sure of only one thing—that the man was a Kanzany. He had nothing about him save a broad-bladed battle knife which Thoric threw to the ground in disgust. The man was dead.

Thoric walked over to Micolai, who was himself bent over his fallen adversary. "Did he have anything on him?"

"No," said Micolai, shivering as he made his reply.

"You acted swiftly there," said Thoric appreciatively. "I would never have expected it of you."

"I too have no idea how it came about," said Micolai still shaking. Inwardly, however, he was warmed by the barbarian's words of approbation, and the icy fingers clutching at his heart began to relax their grip. "I simply raised my weapon in self-defense. My knife must have caught him full in the throat."

He felt the motionless figure's neck. When he

continued, there was astonishment in his voice: "His throat is untouched . . . just a little cut in his cheek, nothing else . . . Thoric!" he cried.

"Quiet!" warned the latter.

"The poison works! The sorcerer was right . . ." whispered Micolai excitedly.

"Perhaps. Now, come with me," Thoric urged. "There is not much left of the night."

The Kanzany got up, suddenly filled with a sense of fearlessness. Aha, anybody could come along now, he would stand guard at the gate and anyone who came too close would feel his dagger! A great mound of sleeping bodies would tower up around him!

The Southerner plucked at his sleeve. "Come on now."

"What about him, he will freeze to death?"

"That would be bad luck for him, but I suspect his friend will come back and take care of him. As for the dead one, we shall take him with us. Come, get hold of his legs."

Micolai helped him lift the corpse. Thoric made to throw the cadaver over his shoulder, but the thought of specks of blood dappling his polar-bear skin soon made him reconsider.

"Take his legs and lead on," he ordered. He himself took the dead man's arms, and for a while they carried the body like that, until the Kanzany suddenly let it fall from his arms.

"I cannot go on! I am no longer cold, that is certain, but I shall carry this corpse not a step farther. If you mean to hide it, in the snow here is as good a place as any. . . ."

"He is to be a present for the guards," explained Thoric. "Pick him up, it is not far now."

Ill-humoredly, Micolai picked up the man's legs once more. The latter part of the journey seemed endless to him, but Thoric pushed him onward, and he had to concentrate because of the treacherous ground underfoot. Eventually they reached the wall of the palace garden, unchallenged. Anybody foolhardy enough to try storming these walls would soon lose the desire. Thoric broke into a grin, striding up and down the length of the walls on the Kanzany's heels. Suddenly, from nowhere, there appeared before them two men clad in the mail shirt and red jerkin of the palace guard.

"Halt!" The gleaming sword in the hand of one of them served to emphasize the command. The other one also had his hand on the hilt of his weapon.

Micolai cast Thoric a questioning glance. The latter placed the corpse on the ground, and the Kanzany, breathing a sigh of relief, followed suit, even though alarm was clutching at his heart now that the moment of decision was at hand.

"Who is this?" The guard pointed at the corpse. "Where were you planning to take him?"

"Who *was* this, you mean," replied Micolai in a surge of grim humor, hand sliding unobtrusively toward his dagger. "He is dead, to be precise, and. . . ."

"We found him in the snow, two hundred paces back there," intoned Thoric who had moved to Micolai's side.

"Dead, you say?" The guard nudged the lifeless form with his foot.

Micolai nodded fiercely, feeling the handle of his dagger in his hand. Out of the corner of his eye he saw that the southerner had gripped his sword.

"And what do you intend doing with him?"

"We were bringing him to you," declared Thoric, grinning at the look of surprise on the faces of the two guards.

"To us? What are we supposed to do with him?"

"That is your affair," stated Thoric decisively.

"We merely found him—it is up to you to worry about what to do with him."

"It is a trick, SasPin," snarled the second sentry who had not spoken until that moment. "They probably did the fellow in themselves and are now playing the innocents."

"Do we look the sort to do that?" exclaimed Micolai angrily.

"I am not sure," opined the one who had been addressed as SasPin. "Come on now, take him outside the city and bury him. And do not let us see you around here again!"

"He is staying here!" replied Thoric, and he tried to push past the guard. Micolai joined him.

The sentries raised their swords to bar the way.

"Take him with you!" SasPin ordered menacingly.

Thoric shook his head. "He is yours, my friends," he said, drawing his sword. "You wanted no arguments, I believe?"

"Only if you choose to avoid one, foreigner!" He swung his curved sword at Thoric's head. The latter swayed aside, and lunged with his own long sword. He had aimed his blow at the sentry's legs, and it was with satisfaction that he felt his sword strike home. The other sentry came rushing at him in a frenzy, and Thoric had no time to stand and observe the effect of his action. As he parried the guard's blow, he saw Micolai thrust his dagger into his assailant's sword arm. The latter collapsed without a sound.

"It works," murmured Micolai with a grin. His teeth shone white in the feeble light.

"Good," replied Thoric, and he began to drag the two motionless sentries and the corpse through the gate into the garden.

"If they do wake up, they will tell a very strange tale about a corpse, and they will not suspect that we simply wanted to get into the palace. There, take SasPin's clothes . . . and hurry!"

As Micolai changed his clothes, Thoric went and trampled down the snow in front of the gate, to remove any telltale signs of a fight. More snow was falling in tiny crystal flakes, and by morning it would have hidden everything. All around there was nothing but the silence of a winter's night in the mountains.

At length, Micolai reappeared, clad in the sentry's red jerkin.

"What now?"

"Can you see that faint glimmer over there?"

The Kanzany nodded.

"That must be the sentries' hut. There is one by every gate. We shall take them there. Come on, quick—help me!"

They took hold of the two bodies and dragged them through the snow. They approached the hut with caution. It was a crude dwelling constructed of roughly hewn tree trunks. Thoric listened at the door. He could hear the crackling of a fire, and footsteps.

"There is movement in there," he whispered.

"How many occupants are there?" asked Micolai.

Thoric shrugged and listened once more. "One," he said eventually, with certainty in his voice.

Micolai nodded, and pulled the helmet right down over his face. He had pushed the door open before Thoric could stop him.

"We have a corpse out here. What should we do with it?" he said in a voice apparently hoarse with the cold. He raised his hands in front of his face as though he were warming them with his breath.

"A corpse? Where?" The foreign tones resounded in Thoric's ear.

"Outside. Come with me!"

Thoric pressed himself against the wall of the hut as the door swung open and Micolai appeared, closely followed by a Kanzany in sentry's uniform. As the latter bent over the two lifeless bodies, Thoric grabbed him from behind and Micolai thrust his dagger into the man's calf. Their victim collapsed instantaneously. Micolai broke into a grin.

Thoric returned the grin, but offered a word of warning: "This magic potion of yours is making you bold, shopkeeper. Just beware of becoming too bold!"

Micolai nodded. The moment of tension passed, and he felt himself beginning to shiver once more. "Have no fear of that," he murmured bravely.

"Let us get them into the hut, and then you must go back to the gate. Hang on there as long as you can. But remember—your magic dagger will not hold off a whole troop of soldiers. Get away from there quickly when the time comes, understood?"

"Yes, barbarian. Now, what about SiShin?"

"I shall take her to SasKan's house. Meet me there before nightfall tonight. And bring the gold with you!" With a light chuckle, he disappeared into the night.

Micolai listened to the diminishing sound of his footsteps. The cold plucked at his body with fingers of ice. He was now all alone in the dark. He stared down at the motionless bodies at his feet. What had he let himself in for?

# 9

Thoric followed the narrow but well-trodden path until the building reared up huge and black in front of him. He could see hardly a thing. That which was not concealed in darkness was veiled by the heavily falling snow. When he saw another sentry standing ahead of him he knew that he had to be right by the wall. Thoric ventured a few paces nearer, trusting that the sentry could see no better than he. He could now make out the vague outline of a gate, and he stopped to listen. Nothing moved. He bent down and took a handful of snow which he squeezed into a tight snowball. He threw it. It struck the gate with a hollow thud. He held his breath.

Nothing. Cautiously, he stood up and walked toward the gate. No one made any attempt to bar his way. The iron-clad door was, however, locked.

Thoric glanced around him. On both sides of the gate the smooth stone walls towered up into the sky. It was impossible to scale them. He decided to walk a little farther on, but suddenly stopped when he heard voices. Just then the gate flew open, as if someone had given it a kick. A man came out, a jug in one hand and a tray in the other. He looked neither left nor right, but simply strode, shoulders hunched, toward the sentry post.

Thoric drew his sword automatically but made no move. This was a job for the shopkeeper. As the man entered the hut, Thoric thought he heard a cry, but the snow-heavy air muffled all sound. He waited a moment longer, but silence continued to reign. "Good work, shopkeeper," he murmured to himself.

Then he walked through the open gate, closing it behind him. The atmosphere was warm and stuffy, and heavy with the smell of food. The kitchens had to be nearby. His eyes had become accustomed to the dark, and he could make out the lighter crescent of the heavens not far away. He strode toward it, and shortly came to a tiny forecourt redolent with the typical smell of stables. Twenty paces farther on there was another passageway from which there emanated torchlight.

Thoric slunk noiselessly from one wall to the next, looking out onto the snow-covered square, the far end of which was lost in darkness. Nothing was to be seen save the flicker of the torches on either side of the entrances into the palace building itself, and light shining from the numerous windows. The sound of voices was to be heard. Then, to his right, the more highly pitched laugh of a woman rang out. It came from one of the windows bathed in light. Thoric pressed himself hard to the cold wall as the silhouette of a woman suddenly appeared. His gaze wandered upward from the window and then, by its dark shape revealed in the starlight, he realized he was looking at the tower.

He waited patiently until the woman's outline disappeared. Then he ran, half-crouching, along the wall until he reached the entrance, a heavy door behind which he could hear the indistinct sounds of men's voices.

The Kanzany had been right. This was where the sentries were—and this was where he had to get in! But how?

How many men might there be in there? He had only one certain advantage: they were hardly likely to kill him! They would try to capture him alive and take him before HalJin. Ought he to rely on the probability that the blue substance on his sword would have the desired effect? Of course, he had seen it work with Micolai's dagger but . . . his long-standing mistrust of anything connected with wizardry made him doubtful. However, there was no time to lose. He drew the sword. Cursed be the hazzonish sorcerer if it went awry!

Just for a fleeting moment he tried to imagine that he was standing before this door without the magical substance. What would he do in those circumstances? He shrugged his shoulders. Just what he was going to do anyway!

He looked around him. There was nobody near the tower. "Bring on the yellow-skinned heathen!" he muttered, and banged on the door with the handle of his sword. Inside, the chatter came to an abrupt halt. Footsteps approached the door. With a gentle movement, Thoric lightly drew the cutting edge of his sword across the back of the hand that had opened the door.

The Kanzany uttered a curse, let go of the door-handle and clutched at his hand. A moment later he sank to the floor. Five men leapt from a bench and grabbed their weapons. Thoric dashed into the room and closed the door behind him. Without giving his opponents a moment's respite he came rushing at them. The torchlight shone brightly in the low-ceilinged room. For a moment the men stared in terror at the blue blade in the hand of the yellow-haired devil who had suddenly appeared in their midst. Two of them felt the bite of this blade, one in the shoulder, the other in the leg. They sank to the ground, even before the amazement had left their faces.

"Stop! Where do you think you are going?" growled Thoric as another of them made for the door. The tip of the sword licked out toward the man's arm and seemed barely to touch him. Nonetheless, the Kanzany collapsed without uttering a sound. The two remaining guards stared in horror at this magic sword whose merest touch brought death.

They threw their own weapons down and ran off up into the tower. Thoric followed them up a steep winding staircase. The wood creaked underfoot, and the hurried footsteps echoed loudly round the whole building. Thoric caught one of them on the foot, bringing him down. His cry died away instantly.

A nearby wooden door was flung open. Thoric was confronted by the face of a girl, pale with fright; but only for a moment, as the door closed with a bang and the bolt was shot home. Thoric hurried on, cursing. Now he had to be quick, before they could find some way of alerting the world outside of the tower. There was no doubt in his mind but that the girl was one of the Prince's ladies.

A little higher up, the staircase came to an end. The sentry ran in desperation up to the archer's station, just as Thoric reached the top story.

"Up here! Up here!" the man bellowed into the night. "Help! It is the devil himself! Up. . . !"

"Here I am," gasped Thoric. He hit the man on the back with the flat of his sword, forcing all the air from his lungs, and then he nicked him on the back of the neck with the edge of the blade. "Sleep soundly!"

Now where? The girl had to be up here somewhere.

"SiShin!" he cried, but not at the top of his voice.

Immediately there came an answer—fists drummed against a door to his right, and a muffled voice cried out, "In here! In here!"

Thoric felt along the wall in the darkness and came upon a great bolt. He pulled it back. The door sprang open and the girl came running out toward him. He caught her on the arm with his half-raised sword.

"Ye gods!" cried Thoric as the girl collapsed. "Anything but that!"

But it was already done. With a sigh, Thoric knelt to take a closer look at the wound. Just the merest nick on the underside of her arm! The fates were obviously mocking him. Anyway, now for a rapid withdrawal. He slapped the girl's face gently two or three times but he knew in his heart that it was pointless. A noise on the stairs caught his attention.

A shadow came padding toward him. He raised his sword in self-defense.

"Do not strike me," came the breathless whisper of a girl's voice.

"Then stay where you are!" ordered Thoric. "Who are you?"

"I am TayaSar, bold stranger. I am the Prince's sister. I wish to get away from here. Take me with you!"

"Show me your hands," snarled Thoric, who was striving in vain to pierce the blackness to see whether she was carrying a weapon.

"There they are, foreigner. They are empty." She took a pace forward. Starlight shone through the narrow slit in the battlements onto her white hands and pale face.

"What am I to do with you? This other one is already burden enough." He pointed down at the lifeless bundle on the floor, lost in feverish thought. The Prince would have him hung, drawn and quartered if he were captured. On the other hand, the girl might serve as protection for the return journey—and as a hostage.

Her arms were suddenly round his neck. Her mouth slipped hotly across his cheek. "Quick!" she whispered.

Excited voices came from below them, shocking Thoric out of his immobility. "Too late!" he muttered.

"Not yet it isn't! Come!" She ran down the stairs.

Thoric picked up the lifeless form of SiShin and threw it over his shoulder like a sack. As he ran along behind the girl, he realized that he was caught in a trap. The tower was a prison. They could either drag him out of there by force or else starve him out. The latter was more likely. He could not possibly hope to put the entire palace to sleep, even if his arm were never to grow tired. Whatever designs TayaSar might have on him, she was his only salvation. Pretty name that, TayaSar.

Her face suddenly appeared before him. "In here!"

There was an open door. The southerner stumbled through it with his burden. Before the bolt clanged home he thought he could hear voices, men's voices, and they were approaching rapidly.

The room was bright and expensively furnished, with heavy draperies, silk coverlets and thick-pile carpets. Thoric let his load slide to the floor as the girl went and snuffed out a number of candles. TayaSar slipped out of her shimmering cloak and threw it carelessly onto the bed. Then she piled up the coverlets onto one side of the bed and motioned Thoric to bring the girl over.

Thoric lifted the unconscious girl onto the bed and together they pulled the coverlets back over her. Outside, the wooden staircase was creaking under the heavy footsteps of men running.

Thoric leaped to his feet and hid behind the door. TayaSar stayed by the bed, and began to peel off her outer garments. She smiled when she intercepted Thoric's gaze, but continued to remove her clothing without false modesty. She lowered her head and began to undo the fastenings of her silk underclothes. Thoric felt an unexpected surge of warmth, and was unable to turn his eyes away. He could see the laughter in her dark eyes, the sweet mockery in the corners of her mouth at the exciting effect of her actions, the tinge of a red blush in her young face which gave the lie to her otherwise perfectly simulated shamelessness.

Then the footsteps came clattering up to the door, and Thoric held his breath. Suppose the little beast were to betray him. . . ! She let the last undergarment fall to the floor just as the door flew open. Thoric caught a glimpse of her firm breasts, and then the door blocked his field of vision. The girl let out a sharp cry, and a surprised man's voice cried out. "Princess!"

"Commandant! What do you mean by this outrage!" she shouted angrily.

The door was hastily slammed shut once more.

"A thousand pardons, Princess. I . . . we . . . are looking for a man. . . ." The voice trailed off.

"In my room?" cried the girl in a new fit of rage. She went on, furiously, "You would like it to be so, would you not? If this is another of my brother's tricks. . . !"

"Please forgive me, Princess," replied the commander embarrassed. "Please get dressed; I must search your room. My orders are to inspect every room, without exception . . ."

The girl cast Thoric an anxious glance. He nodded back at her calmly.

"Can you hear me, Princess? The man is dangerous, and he must still be in the tower. If you do not open this door . . ." the commander hesitated, "then I shall be obliged to order my men to enter by force. . . ."

"Very well, commandant. I know that you are merely carrying out my charming brother's orders. Please, wait just a moment. . . ." She gathered up her underclothes and rapidly did up the fastenings; then she slipped into her outer garments, and cast Thoric a questioning glance.

The latter raised his sword ready to strike and gestured to her to open up. Pale-faced, she walked to the door and opened it.

"Commandant!"

"Ah, Princess, I am pleased that you have not made my duty more difficult to carry out than it already is." The commandant came into the room, noticed the pile of coverlets and walked toward it. "What is this. . . . ?"

Thoric slipped in behind him and jabbed him with his sword in the hollow of the knee, which was not protected by his mail-shirt. The commandant spun round and stared at Thoric for what seemed an eternity. Fury flashed in his eyes, and was snuffed out in all-embracing drowsiness. He fell backward onto the girl asleep under the coverlets.

TayaSar surveyed Thoric in some confusion. "Sorcery!" she cried. "Is he dead?"

Thoric shook his head. "No, Princess. He is merely sleeping, like the girl."

Her eyes widened. "You touched her with the sword too?"

Thoric broke into a grin. "The commandant was just saying how dangerous I am . . ." His face suddenly became serious. "We must get him out of your room—his men will come looking for him."

Princess TayaSar had turned pale. She was the victim of her own courage. She was putting her safety in the hands of a foreigner who might, indeed, be the very devil himself. His face suddenly looked ugly to her, and the blue sword was a sure sign that there was something unnatural afoot. However, she had come to no harm so far, and the prospect of escaping from the clutches of her brother and his wedding plans for her was attractive indeed. And once she was out of the palace. . . .

She shook her head. "We must stay here no longer. More men will be coming. And just as soon as my brother hears of this he will send whole armies marching on the tower. His sister's honor," she stamped her foot angrily, "and the chance to indulge his whims will be more than he is able to deny himself. I know that. The commandant will already have sent a messenger off to HalJin, that is certain." The very thought of it caused her to wring her hands. "If you value your own skin, stranger, I beg you to make haste." She pulled the coverlets back and started to lift the girl from the bed.

Thoric needed no second bidding. He went to help her, taking the girl on his shoulder. TayaSar threw her cloak about her shoulders and opened the door cautiously. From higher up the staircase came the sound of footsteps, and from below, the sound of voices. She bit her lip, and looked earnestly at Thoric.

"Now is as good a time as any," he muttered. They ran down the stairs, insofar as the steep, narrow steps would permit. Instantly, further hurried footsteps echoed from above. Ahead of him, the Princess appeared to be flying, her dark cloak fluttering like a pair of devil's wings in the flickering light. Thoric followed, hard on her heels.

There were more than a dozen men in the guard room. They stood aside when the Princess suddenly appeared.

"Up there!" she cried. "He is still up there!"

Thoric kept his face hidden behind his load, insofar as he was able.

The confusion lasted only a few seconds, but by the time the first cries of anger were uttered, Thoric had already reached the door. Thoric succeeded in stumbling through the door out into the open and slamming it behind him. Their pursuers thumped on the oak panels of the door, and a broadside of Kanzany oaths accompanied the Tanilorner as he ran out into the darkness of the square. TayaSar came scurrying along just behind him, her cloak billowing out behind her. She stopped when she reached the dark end of the square.

The door into the tower flew open. Soldiers came dashing out into the open like a swarm of angry hornets. On the other side of the square, the palace building came suddenly to life, men came rushing out into the darkened square carrying torches, and long tongues of light licked out across the gleaming snow.

"Princess!" cried Thoric. "Princess!"

She stopped. He let his bundle fall to the ground in front of him.

"A friend is waiting for me at the East Gate. Quickly!" he rasped.

He turned and ran back toward the light of the torches, and his pursuers.

They came to a halt when they saw him coming. Some three dozen of the little yellow-faced palace guards stared at him, eyes sparkling feverishly. A goodly number of them slipped in behind him to cut off his escape.

They were carrying no weapons. They wanted him alive!

He smiled a grim smile.

"Sweet dreams," he muttered, hoping that his merchant friend was still guarding the gate. It seemed an eternity since he had left him.

The ring of red jerkins began to close in on him. There was no escape now, but there was going to be a Big Sleep, or his name was not Thoric of Tanilorn!

"Good luck, Princess!" he said under his breath, and took a firmer grip on his sword.

The men's hands were balled into fists, and their eyes were fixed hungrily on him, as if yearning to drown some of the monotony of palace life in a few powerful blows.

Before they could close the circle completely,

their oppressed victim suddenly leapt in among them. His sword darted and flicked at their bodies like the twinkling tongue of some serpent.

Then, suddenly, there were three of them hanging on to his arm, and several on his back; another clawed at his hair. Yet another grabbed his sword and wrested it from his grasp.

He fell to the ground under the weight of bodies. The snow was suffocating him.

# 10

Micolai pressed himself into the shadow of the great gate. A cold wind was whistling along the wall, blowing the snow into small drifts in its path. Of the two men's tracks there was already no sign. The air was filled with a gentle whistling sound, and the stone houses in the distance sat there like squat black dwarves in the winter desolation. No unusual noises were to be heard emanating from the palace. So, they had not yet discovered the presence of the Tanilorner.

He fought back the desire to go and spend a few moments in the guard-hut to warm himself; after all, Thoric was relying on him to watch here, and he would be pleased with him. He had dealt without fuss with the lad from the kitchens, who now lay in the locked hut alongside the others.

Micolai was somewhat amused at his own courage and resolve. However, the easy and effortless way everything had passed off, and the sure knowledge that rather than killing them, he was dealing with his adversaries without the use of force, by a magical trick, did however cause him temporarily to forget that these adversaries did not fight by the same methods, and they would certainly not be much bothered about sparing his life. It was all rather akin to some absorbing game, and not bloody reality. The very fact that he, a simple merchant from Sambun, should be standing guard at the gate of the Prince's palace was itself absurd enough to foster this feeling of unreality in him. And what about this courage of his, then? Well, just let them come . . . .

They came.

A black serpent slunk away from the line of dark houses, advancing directly on the gate. Alarm began to creep into Micolai's heart, culminating in the conviction that he should have disappeared hours before.

The group coming his way was the midnight patrol—a dozen soldiers fully armed and proud of their prowess in battle. Why had he not thought of it before? Every night they patrolled the streets of the city, and along the walls. He cursed himself, and Southern barbarians in general. Anyway, the disappearance time of which Thoric had spoken was here. . . . Or . . .?

An idea flashed through his head which made him shiver, an idea such as even hard-boiled old warhorses would have considered pure madness, the idea of a crass fool. And yet. . . .

Then he saw that it was already too late to run away. He could hear the gentle rattle of their weapons and mail shirts quite distinctly, and he could clearly see their faces, pale beneath their helmets.

Then the patrol had reached him, and Micolai

thanked the gods that it was night and dark enough to conceal his trembling. The commander of the troop gave the order to halt. He stared at the gate, and then at the guard. Micolai struggled desperately to fight down the feelings of numb terror within him. As the commander made to walk toward him, he cried out: "Come not a step nearer! This is your first and final warning!" He pulled out his dagger.

"What are you playing at?" the commander began, reaching for his sword. "Give the password!"

*Password? The game is up,* was the thought that flashed through the merchant's mind. Then, firmly, he said, "No, I shall not betray the secret password to you. Who knows, you may well be one of them."

"Idiot!" the commandant interjected. "Can you not see that we are the patrol?" He gestured toward his men, who were standing expectantly a little way behind him.

"Perhaps," declared Micolai, "perhaps not. You could be in these men's power." He whispered the words firmly.

"I could what?" exclaimed the commandant, totally bewildered. He stood and stared at the merchant as though at one of the snow dwarves who people claimed lived up in the mountains, watching over the pillars of hanging ice.

"Can you not see," he said at last, hoarsely yet in an odd whisper, "that these men are the Prince's soldiers?"

"They look as though they are," said Micolai. "But you shall not pass this gate until I am sure of it."

"What else could they be, you lunatic!" he cried, turning to face his men. "Do you hear what this. . . ?"

"Quiet!" cried Micolai, so urgently that the commandant broke off in surprise. "They might be demons—and they would not be the first to show up here tonight."

The commandant laughed out loud. "Demons, you say, my men. . . ?"

"Quiet!" cried Micolai once more. "For the sake of the gods, be still! It was only a short while ago that they arrived, men just like you or me, a smile on their faces, a friendly word. And they wanted to come through this gate." He tried to make his voice heavy with horror, and found it not difficult. He had gone cold all over. "We tried to resist. There was a fearful struggle. My colleague is dead—there, see for yourself." He opened the gate a trifle and pointed to the body of the would-be assassin, which he had dragged here with the southerner. As the commandant came closer, Micolai backed away, raising his dagger in a gesture of defense. "Keep away from me!" he shouted in obvious terror.

The commandant halted involuntarily, now a little uncertain himself. "Where did they go?"

"We managed to overpower them," replied Micolai. "They are locked up in the hut." He went on, as though quaking with terror: "They are not dead, and yet their hearts still beat. They seem simply to be asleep, and yet nothing wakes them. . . ." He broke off when he saw the disbelief vanish from the commandant's face, and he noticed the uncertainty in his eyes. It would be dangerous to push it too hard. . . .

"Show me them!" demanded the commandant. A little of Micolai's terror could now be heard in his voice also.

"Not before I know how I stand with you!" said

Micolai firmly. "You could still be one of them. . . ."

"And who is to say that *you* are not one of them?"

"Look at this dagger!" The merchant raised it, and its blue sheen was clearly visible in the feeble starlight.

"What about it?"

"I got it from a wizard up in the far north. I always carry it with me. It was only thanks to this that I was able to overcome the demons, and through it I can tell whether I am dealing with a man of flesh and blood or not. Here," he held his arm up and nicked his wrist with the top of the blade, where a tiny part of the metal had escaped the liquid's touch. Blood oozed from the cut, and for a moment he was afraid that he might fall asleep. But nothing happened. "And now, commandant, give me your arm!"

The latter hesitated.

"You hesitate?" cried Micolai triumphantly.

"Nonsense," growled the commandant, reaching out his arm.

The merchant touched him with that same area of the blade. From the scratch he inflicted came a drop of blood. Micolai breathed a sigh of obvious relief. "Which of these men can you trust?"

"TseGwan, my deputy."

"Call him over."

At the commandant's behest, one of the men detached himself from the group and came over to the gate.

"TseGwan," the commandant began. Micolai raised a warning finger to his lips. The commandant sighed. "Hold out your arm, TseGwan."

The latter held out his arm to Micolai as ordered; he gave a start when he saw the blue knife.

However, the merchant kept a firm grip on his arm. A moment later TseGwan sank to the snow-covered ground and lay there motionless.

"He is one of them," breathed Micolai. *One less to worry about, that was easy enough,* he thought.

The commandant bent incredulously over the sleeping form of his deputy. "TseGwan!" he cried, shaking the motionless figure.

"He is not TseGwan, at least, not anymore," murmured Micolai. "It is just a demon in TseGwan's body." He bent down. "Place your hand on his chest, you will feel his heart beating. But it is not his blood that drives it, it is the terrifying strength bestowed on the dead. Look, no blood is coming from the cut." He lifted the man's arm.

When the commandant stood up again he was ashen-faced.

"How many of the others are also like him?" he muttered in fury.

Micolai shrugged his shoulders. *Do not overdo it,* he thought. *Ye gods, let caution prevail.*

"We must find out," he stated calmly.

The commandant nodded, fists clenched.

"And before they discover what we are doing, too," continued Micolai. "They wish to get into the palace for some reason. The life of the Prince himself is in danger. We must be careful. The knife test removes all doubt. So, as long as they remain unsuspecting let us allow the knife to decide."

The commandant nodded once more. He drew his sword. The fate of his deputy seemed to have filled him with impotent rage. The result which Micolai had scarcely dared hope for had come about—the commandant had become his ally. The slightest suspicious move, and he would be fighting his own men. Nonetheless, Micolai was not yet disposed to relax. The hairs on the back of his neck bristled at the thought that everything could yet go awry.

"Call each of them over in turn," he whispered. "But let us stand on the other side of the gate. They might become suspicious if they were to see someone else collapse—if they have not already done so . . ."

The commandant called them over, sword raised, and saw to it that they stretched out their arm and remained still while Micolai went to work with his blue knife.

Four of them sank into the snow and lay motionless. The commandant's face grew more and more pale with every one that fell. Micolai expected at any moment to see disbelief creep into the pale features, into the eyes, and his heart skipped a beat with every victim that fell. However, to the fifth he did nothing.

"K'ang!" exclaimed the man when he learned of what was going on.

"It was only midnight that I was drinking wine with TorSung in GisRin's tavern. He was frightened of something, but he did not know what . . ."

Fate seems to be playing into my hands, thought Micolai. The gods truly mean to be good to me. Their desires from the other world were satisfied with the fear that he was feeling, the thudding of his heart, the secret remorse at his sins. It seemed to him almost as if they were taking pleasure in the crazy things that were happening, and were in fact keeping a sheltering hand over him.

The men came through the gate quite unsuspecting, but the way they recoiled from the glistening blue blade already looked like an indication of guilt to the commandant. Five more of them fell into magical slumber. The sixth and last seemed calm and collected, although somewhat bewildered. Micolai dared do no more than that, and so of the dozen there remained three.

Micolai put the knife away with obvious relief.

"We must warn the Prince," the commandant declared. Micolai saw him tremble, although he was not sure if it was out of horror or helpless rage. He shuddered. His skin was not yet saved.

"Kir-Dvas, stay here at the gate with him. And let no one through, whoever it may be!"

Micolai nodded. The commandant and the second man disappeared into the darkness of the palace garden. Micolai was less than happy to see them go. How much time was left him? And where, by Arull, was the yellow-haired barbarian?

Despite the snow, he had the feeling that the ground was growing warm beneath his feet. The desire to run away was almost overwhelming. Had he not after all accomplished something almost superhuman? He had wiped out the feared midnight patrol, which would earn him the eternal gratitude of the thieves' guild, if nothing else.

He heaved a sigh. He was already a respected gentleman in his new profession, for as a merchant he would henceforth have to renounce any thought of taking part in the life of Sambun. It was true that it was dark and that the helmet did most of the rest, but even with KuaYin himself on his side it might not be enough if one of the men should ever recognize him again. No, the days of the merchant's prosperity and respectability were over; nothing could change that.

Where by all the gods was that damned barbarian?

"Listen!" hissed Kir-Dvas suddenly.

He spun round, startled. Footsteps could be heard crunching through the snow, accompanied by heavy gasping noises and the sound of something being dragged. For a moment there was nothing to be seen, and Micolai, who was far from having no fear of demons, stood and stared in horror. Kir-Dvas was also motionless.

A misshapen figure emerged, staggering across the snow up to the gate, gasping for breath. Micolai's hand closed round his dagger.

Suddenly, the figure's misshapenness resolved itself into two parts, one part sliding away from the other and crashing to the ground. The other part, the part which had been doing the carrying, spoke in a surprisingly clear female voice: "Are you the friends of the barbarian? Here is SiShin. Take me . . . with . . . you. . . ." The figure collapsed in exhaustion.

Micolai's thoughts raced. He had to get Kir-Dvas out of the way. Out loud, he said "Yes, we are they."

"What barbarian?" asked Kir-Dvas suspiciously. "I am friendly with no barbarians. . . . Who are you?" He bent over the exhausted figure. Micolai took advantage of the moment to thrust the dagger into the back of the man's neck. Micolai pushed him aside as he fell.

"He has been working for us," declared Micolai, "only he did not know it. Who are you? And where is Thoric?"

The girl let the hood of her cloak fall away, and a face became visible in the starlight.

"The Prince's sister!" exclaimed Micolai. "Where is Thoric?"

"Listen!" she warned.

He could hear it very faintly. The sounds of a struggle, and then silence.

"They have him," he whispered.

She nodded, exhausted. She tried to lift the lifeless figure of the girl to her feet. "SiShin," she gasped, "we must get to SasKan's house."

Micolai sighed. These barbarians shrank from nothing! The Prince's sister!

He had to get the girl away. A long way away! Ah, the very thought of it!

Prince HalJin would not kill the barbarian, at least not immediately. Not until he had his sister back. And he, Micolai, would see to it that he did not get his sister back that quickly.

# 11

The man seated on the marble throne was a Kanzany, stocky, black-haired and dark-skinned; prominent cheekbones and a strong yellow pigmentation showed him to be from the highlands. Dozens of tribes of such people lived in the mountains of Batarak, to the North of the Assu. He was, however, corpulent by comparison with the muscular palace guards. The Prince's red cloak, adorned with the emblem of the falcon, hung in folds around him, but it could not conceal his obesity.

He was HalJin, the Reyah, Prince of Sambun, ruler of the city and its hinterland down as far as the hilly region by the hazzonish border. He controlled the only merchant route into the highlands of Arullu. This made Sambun a very rich city and HalJin the most powerful and influential prince in all the highlands. However, he was also renowned for another thing—he had succeeded in creating a comfortable merchant route to the sea, passing through hazzonish territory. Regular patrols of troops threw the Hazzonish defenses farther and farther back.

HalJin knew that sooner or later it would come to an open conflict, but he could feel certain of the support and consent of the court, since the seat of the court, although well-defended, lay on the other side of Arullu, astride the most profitable merchant route, in that it was the shortest to take goods north. Southerners no longer needed to take the lengthy route over Movus. HalJin also prized it highly personally, because it meant that he was the first to see goods and treasures from the south and could thus take his pick.

Two incidents occurred to interrupt his cogitations. The lute player to his left suddenly hit a false note, and one of the two dancers stumbled.

He smiled as the red-haired girl resumed her dance step, but turning to the minstrel, he said, "You are playing out of tune, my dear fellow. Perhaps you would prefer to dance?"

The lute player hit another wrong note, and put his instrument down. His youthful face was pale, and his dark eyes betrayed fear. "Dance, my Prince?" he asked uncomprehendingly.

HalJin nodded. "Like those two. Take a close look at them." He pointed toward the two dancers who had also stopped, and were standing there exhausted.

"No," stammered the minstrel, "I am not a girl. You would surely find little amusement in my. . . ."

"Perhaps more than in your lute-playing." said HalJin with a grin. The idea seemed to exhilarate him.

"No! I do not know how to dance," croaked the musician.

"It can be learned," stated the Prince mischievously, a heavy note of mockery in his voice. "Sit down! Your predecessor was also inclined to play out of key. Even more often than you. . . . Do you know what happened to him, SaiTeh?"

The minstrel shook his head, pushing the dark locks out of his eyes. He seemed to have grown even paler. Never had he regretted so deeply that fateful decision to come to the court of the Prince as he did at that moment.

The Prince laughed. "He learned to dance." He signaled to one of the dancers. "Take your dress off!"

The latter obeyed, and SaiTeh's eyes widened. The dancer undid the fastenings of the glittering gown, which was made of ankle-length green silk veils. There was no sign of breasts, no sleek girl's thigh.

"This is your predecessor," explained HalJin. "He is a better dancer than many of the girls. . . ."

The lute-player swallowed hard. "Why does he wear a dress?"

"Because I am not very keen on male dancers," continued HalJin with a smile. "A concession on his part, although not entirely of his own free will. . . ." He gave the dancer a signal, and the latter put his dress back on.

"What about . . . the other one?"

"Oh, the other one is genuine, aren't you, my pretty one?" The girl blushed, and nodded.

The Prince turned once more to the still-shocked SaiTeh. "And now play, my little string-plucker—and keep in tune, or you will be dancing in the market-place in three days' time to celebrate the Feast of the Sun." He laughed out loud at the sight of the pale, horror-stricken face of the minstrel.

Then, with an impatient gesture, he said, "Play us a jolly tune, lute player. How am I supposed to get on with my meditating with you playing false notes? And you, my beauties, show your legs. Come on! Come on!" He clapped in time to the music and sank back into his reverie, while the minstrel plucked at his strings in mortal dread.

SaiTeh's heart was overcome with a flood of joy and relief when a knock came at the door and HalJin bade the visitor enter. He had cramp in the fingers, and for the last few minutes the only thing that had driven him on was the thought of having to dance. The two dancers also stopped, and sank exhausted onto the steps leading up to the podium on which the throne stood.

"Come in, ChuenGoch!"

A Kanzany wearing the red uniform of the palace guard entered and raised a hand in greeting. "The sorcerer is here!"

HalJin leaped to his feet and rubbed his hands together. "Good! Show him in. No! Wait! We need more light. First light the candle along the walls, but not the oil lamps from Wolsany—they stink. Ah yes, and you are dismissed for the day. Off with you! Disappear! And be quick about it!"

He gestured to the dancers, who scurried out of the room, heaving a sigh of relief. The minstrel made to go with them and had almost reached the door before the Prince's command rooted him to the spot.

"You stay here! I may have further need of you. Have some wine brought in for him, ChuenGoch. And then we are not to be disturbed!"

ChuenGoch, for many years the Reyah's confidant and commanding officer of the bodyguard, struck SaiTeh as a very odd person. His silent gait, his withdrawn and remote disposition and his ubiquity made him a terrifying figure in the eyes of anyone wishing the Prince ill. Those who were by nature nervous claimed to feel a chill when he was near, a demoniacal aura, but that was merely anxiety clutching with cold hand at their hearts, for there was really nothing very demoniacal about ChuenGoch. All over the palace, however, they knew how quick he was with the dagger, and how high was the Prince's esteem for him.

Immediately, there appeared a maid who brought the minstrel his wine. The latter retreated with it to the darkest corner of the room.

Then the sorcerer entered and hailed the Prince in friendly manner, although with no especial reverence. HalJin returned the greeting in almost exuberant fashion, and the sorcerer sat down on the Princess' throne.

He was no Kanzany, although none could actually say where he did come from. He never mentioned it. He was a very old man, with deep wrinkles in his face. His hair was as white as snow, and yet he was surrounded by an aura of youthful vigor, and he moved with supple gait, unbowed by the usual weariness of the elderly. His clear, pale eyes were filled with a cold unearthly wisdom. He wore a wide cloak made of white wool.

"The snow falling outside this night will be the last of the season, HalJin," he said. His voice had an oddly gentle quality to it. "In a few days, the thaw will send torrents gushing down into the valleys. They are green already, and have been for some time. The first ships await your men."

"They are ready," HalJin assured him. "Enough of them to squash once and for all the delight that these hazzonish dogs take in sudden attacks."

The sorcerer shook his head in warning. "You

must beware. Wolsany troops are gathering in E'lil. They will march north, and a Wolsany fleet is sailing east along Hero Straits. Kimah has already fallen into their hands. Hazzon will offer no resistance—quite the reverse, in fact—they are welcoming the conqueror from the south with open arms. What that means is not difficult to guess—they will feel strong enough to hit you even harder than before, although they will not dare to penetrate openly into the country."

"You mean that Wolsany will attack us?" cried the Prince.

The sorcerer shrugged. "The Lion is under way. Nobody knows quite how strong he might feel himself to be, or where he will stop. That he feels powerful is beyond doubt. And he has a treaty with the northerners."

"K'wan!" exclaimed HalJin. "Does the King know of this?"

The sorcerer nodded. "He is taking counsel. A fleet is sailing at full speed toward Movus to engage the intruder in battle."

"And I. . . ?"

"You will do nothing outrageous. Hold your men in full readiness, but bid them exercise caution. Send out scouts. Send messengers to the outlying villages. Gather the tribes of nomads together. As soon as the snows melt set about fortifying the city."

"But it is already fortified . . ." declared HalJin.

"Inadequately!" the sorcerer admonished him.

"They will never reach these mountains," replied the Prince with some conviction. "They are unaccustomed to the snow and cold, and the cutting winds of the mountains."

"By the time they arrive there will no longer be any snow," the sorcerer objected.

The Reyah paced up and down the room, uneasy.

"I cannot foretell the future," continued the sorcerer. "That is beyond even my powers. But I do know that it is possible that the Wolsany will come up into the mountains—indeed, it is probable, HalJin. You will do well to prepare for that. Call all the highland princes together." After a moment's reflection, he continued: "A messenger is already on his way from Arullu, and he will be here in three days' time. He is bringing orders from the King."

"Do you know what these orders are?"

"Yes," said the sorcerer, nodding. "But you could not follow them yet. Why do you wish to anticipate fate? Your omniscience might be a source of worry to the King. He is already not greatly enamored of your power, as you know!"

"So *you* keep telling me!"

"Do you doubt my word?"

HalJin broke into a grin. "Let us be patient. Come, minstrel, play us a pretty tune!"

SaiTeh pushed his tankard aside and took hold of his lute. A vision of the marketplace in all its festive decoration flashed before his inner eye. He plucked very carefully and deliberately at the strings, and even he himself was moved by the beauty of the sounds that came forth. When he glanced up, he saw the bright eye of the sorcerer trained on him. He felt the goose-pimples climb up his back, although the old man's gaze was not unfriendly.

"Where did you acquire your minstrel, HalJin? He is good."

"Oh?" The Prince awoke with a start from his reverie and began to listen. After a while he broke into a grin, and said, "You are right. He has never played as well as this before."

"And I am filled with admiration for your dancers every time I see them. It is pleasing the way that you patronize the finest exponents of the arts at your court."

"Yes, I do seem to be conducive to the display of talent." HalJin grinned at the musician, who blanched and lowered his head.

"Do you also sing?" asked the wizard.

HalJin turned his head away. "Does he have to?"

"Sing!" ordered the old magician imperiously.

The lute-player strummed a few chords by way of an introduction and then began melodiously to intone one of the monotonous yet compelling ballads typical of Kanzany, concerning a distant race living somewhere in the south. They were ruled over by a cruel king who exploited, tortured and murdered his subjects, and inflicted every injustice on them. One day, however, the dead rose up with the raw savagery of the devil himself to slay the king and his henchmen in horrible manner, thereby releasing the survivors from the yoke.

The sorcerer listened attentively, and even HalJin could not stop himself being charmed by the magical quality and vividness of the performance. When the minstrel had finished, HalJin let out an enthusiastic cry: "I hereby double your stipend, SaiTeh!" and turning to the sorcerer, he said, "I have never let him sing before. I always thought his singing would be as bad as his lute-playing."

"But his lute-playing is anything but bad!"

"Only since just now," said the Prince with a smile.

"Where did you learn that tale?" the sorcerer asked the minstrel.

"Oh, people sing it in E'lil, and in the taverns of Kreos."

"You have been to these places?"

"Yes, my Lord."

"Do you know who the poeple are of whom you were singing?"

The minstrel shook his head. "It is simply an ancient tale—nobody knows who were the first to sing it. But it has great power to it. It captivates both the ear and the heart."

"And yet this people exists. In the south, you say?"

"Do you mean that this king really did become the victim of the dead?" cried HalJin.

The wizard nodded.

"Then there is truth in the ancient legends of our people," murmured the Prince pensively. He suddenly broke into a relieved smile. "For centuries the dead have lain at rest in the soil of Kanzany. That is a good sign. When the head is severed from the body. . . ." He made a slight whistling noise and pretended to cut a swathe with a sword; he held the imaginary severed head in his hand. "Off!" He spread his fingers, and SaiTeh could almost see the skull roll across the floor.

"Down south, you say? Who can wonder at it? I have heard that they tear the heart from the bodies of the dead, and sometimes even of the living . . ." He laughed. "In the west they club one another to death, and in Wolsany they plunge their swords into the heart. Ye gods! Is it any wonder that the dead sometimes come back!"

The sorcerer shook his head. "Races are different one from the other, as are individuals. The elixir of life is not always simply in the head. For many it is their heart or their hands. In Phelea they tell the tale of a woman's hands that sought out her killers and tore them to pieces. Ha! HalJin, you do not know the warmth of the southern sun, the hot-bloodedness, the passion which transcends death itself. . . ."

"Where does this people dwell?" HalJin had become thoughtful once more.

The sorcerer shrugged.

"In Wolsany? In legendary Huascar beyond the sea? In the deserts?" mused HalJin.

"I must be off." The sorcerer rose to his feet.

The Prince looked startled. "But you will be coming back?" The old man nodded.

"When?"

The sorcerer smiled. "The wind will tell you that."

"The wind?" queried the Prince.

The sorcerer was already at the door. "You did not have this many lights burning when I arrived." He raised a hand. His white cloak fluttered in the breeze. All around him candles went out, all of them, even those by the throne which had been burning previously. With a gentle laugh, the figure vanished. A chill wind blew through the room, carrying the smell of glowing candlewick.

SaiTeh gave a shiver. "It is cold," he muttered.

"Yes, it is cold," agreed the Prince, shaking. "These sorcerers come from another world. They have the chill of the Ether about them." He stretched and sat down on his throne. "Play me something, SaiTeh, it will warm your fingers up. This damned winter has already been dragging on far too long." He rested his chin on his hand and pursed his lips as the minstrel picked up his instrument.

"War!" muttered the Prince. "War in Sambun!"

The door flew open and crashed against the stone wall. The Prince leaped to his feet, startled. A powerful gust of wind made the thick windowpanes rattle.

"ChuenGoch!" cried HalJin. "Have you lost your soul to the devil?"

"You will lose yours too," croaked ChuenGoch. "There is somebody in the White Tower!"

"Do not let him out again!" ordered HalJin.

"It has to be a monster," said the commander of the King's bodyguard breathlessly. "All the sentries are dead. The women are in great danger. . . ."

"A monster?" The Prince laughed. "You jest, my good friend and true. What monster would want to get inside the palace?"

ChuenGoch shrugged. "My men are entering the tower at this very moment, and reinforcements are on the way. . . ."

HalJin ran across to a window, still nimble despite his corpulence, and wrenched it open. His eyes were met by a roundelay of torches in the courtyard. The curses and shouts of the sentries reached his ears. The light of the torches fell upon a solitary figure who was standing facing a whole horde of adversaries. He was rapidly surrounded, and a moment later he went down, engulfed by the horde.

"They have got him! Have him brought here!"

A sentry came rushing into the room. "My Prince, that girl, the merchant's daughter—she has disappeared, and . . . and . . ."

"And what?" cried HalJin sharply.

"And TayaSar. She is gone too."

Prince HalJin gave a nod. "The little beast seized the opportunity to follow him."

"No, Excellency," the soldier broke in, "she ran off before him, distracting the soldiers' attention."

"The little serpent!" growled the Prince. "Did they catch her?"

"No, sire. The men were only bothered about the stranger. . . ."

"Idiots!" screeched HalJin. "Still, she will not get far. The men are to find her, even if it takes all night. She cannot leave the palace. She must not. Her marriage to the Prince of Tambun is far too important . . . ah, they are bringing him in now. . . ."

A number of sentries appeared and shoved the prisoner through the door and over in front of the throne. His hands were tied behind his back. The blond hair hung over his face in great strands, matted and stuck together with perspiration. His face itself was criss-crossed with bloody fingernail scratches.

"Cats and women that did that to you, was it?" cried HalJin with a grin.

"If that is what you call your men then you are right," retorted the prisoner in a good Kanzany accent.

HalJin examined him closely. A southerner, no doubt about that. Could it be that they were arriving earlier than the sorcerer had predicted? Unlikely. He was just one of those scoundrels who traveled about the land offering their swords for hire. They would have to learn that that was not without danger in Sambun.

"Do you know whose house this is?"

The prisoner remained silent.

The Kanzany gave a signal. One of the sentries placed his knife at the prisoner's throat.

"Do you know whose house this is?" he repeated.

"Yours," croaked the prisoner.

"And do you know who I am?"

"Prince HalJin."

The Kanzany surveyed him coldly. "I am the law in Sambun. Did you know that too?"

The prisoner nodded.

The Prince gazed incredulously into the distant, almost ugly features of the prisoner whose sun-tanned skin contrasted so starkly with the yellowish complexions of the others present.

"And yet you dare to try to rob me?" He did not appear to expect an answer, for he followed it up instantly: "Where is the girl?"

He received no answer, not even when the sentry gave the knife at the prisoner's throat a little jerk, and pressed harder. Blood oozed from a tiny cut.

"What is your name?"

"Thoric," croaked the prisoner.

"A Wolsany," stated HalJin.

"A Tanilorner," Thoric corrected him.

The Prince gave a little gesture to indicate how trifling the distinction was. "That will make very little difference when war breaks out."

"War? Here?" exclaimed the prisoner.

The Kanzany made no reply. It was beneath his dignity to do so. Instead, he said, "Since you desire my ladies so much, Tanilorner, I shall gratify your lust. Of all the creatures in the palace, you shall hold the one dearest to me in your arms tonight. . . ."

SaiTeh, guessing what the Prince had in mind, let his lute fall to the floor in shock. For a moment a shrill discord echoed round the room.

HalJin smiled. "However, you will have to put up with me as a spectator to your passionate embraces."

The slight tone of mockery in the Prince's voice left the prisoner quite unmoved. He long since knew that his fate was sealed, that he was to die. It had been clear to him from the moment the guards had wrestled him to the ground. It seemed unlikely that the merchant would be able to help him. He hoped for the girl's sake that the Kanzany had stayed at the gate long enough. And what about the Princess? What might she be able to do?

He had seen well enough during the last few months how imaginative people in this part of the world could be when it came to meting out death. He had no illusions. He was to die this very night—perhaps fifty deaths, perhaps a hundred. But there would be a final one, that was for sure.

He was one of those fatalistic people who so patiently bear all the tribulations which weigh them down. But he was prouder than most. Within him he carried the defiance of the Sea of the Endless Ocean that beat against the coastline of Tanilorn, foaming and frothing. He was not paralyzed with fear, even though his death was certain—in fact, it allowed him freedom of action. No longer were there any risks to avoid, and even the merest ghost of a chance might give him a way out—even rapid death on a guard's dagger would be more welcome than whatever else might await him. And, given the chance, he would not die alone. The thought made him smile.

"I shall not disappoint you, HalJin."

"I certainly hope not—I love drama!"

"In my country, we have a saying, O Prince. . . ."

"Beware, Thoric of Tanilorn. Preaching to me has cost many their tongue."

Thoric continued unabashed. "No chains can hold the dead."

The Kanzany turned pale. He gripped the arms of his throne. Several soldiers came and grabbed hold of Thoric, wrestling him to the floor. One of them tried to force a knife between his jaws. The Tanilorner bucked and twisted wildly.

HalJin waved them away. "Leave him! He will be needing his tongue tonight!" But the mocking tone had gone from his voice.

Then his features relaxed once more. His eyes were cold, but a smile played on his lips. "Come," he said, "allow me to show you her of whom I am thinking."

He climbed down from the throne and walked across the room. When he reached the middle, he suddenly stopped and turned to his minstrel. "Do not get lost, my dear fellow—I have a feeling that I shall be needing you again. ChuenGoch, keep an eye on him!" With these words he strode from the room. The guards followed, bringing the prisoner with them.

They went down one story, then two, then three. The air was cold, damp and stale. The narrow passageway had rough-hewn cliff faces for walls, with occasional stone blocks inserted here and there, obviously by human hand. They were underneath the palace.

It was as quiet as the grave save for the sound of the men's footsteps and breathing, the gentle clink of weapons and the crackling of the torches.

Before them, in the flickering light, there stood an iron door.

One of the sentries pulled back the heavy bolt.

Thoric's knees gave way. A familiar pungent odor filled his nose—the odor of reptiles' excrement.

Was this what the Prince had meant when he had spoken of his most beloved creature? Probably. It fitted in completely with the Kanzany mentality—the things they most loved were also the things they most hated in some peculiar way. And there was nothing the Kanzany hated more than these great reddish-black saurians. Deadly enemies since the beginning of time, each lived off the other in no small measure. The Kanzany ate the great reptiles' eggs and flesh and drank their blood in ritual ceremonies. The giant reptiles in turn ate the Kanzany without ceremony, and at any time, except for the winter which they spent sleeping in caves in the cliffs to avoid the cold. In the port of Movus, Thoric had seen young animals the size of a horse; he had heard that fully-grown creatures could reach twice that size, and that no cage could contain them.

But now, as he entered the room on the other side of the iron door, the blood froze in his veins. A row of mighty iron bars divided the room in two. The stench benumbed his senses. Beyond the stakes lay the grandmother of all reptiles, a gigantic animal the size of a hazzonish dragon. The men looked like dwarves in comparison. It lifted its head with a jerk and stared at the visitors with cold, emotionless eyes. The jaws parted, the red tongue flicked out and breath heavy with the stench of putrefaction swept over the men with a whistling sound.

The guards moved nervously as they led their prisoner along the passageway. HalJin himself kept well away although his gaze never left his darling creature, and there was a gleam in his eye. It very shortly became obvious why. With one bound the monster was at the railings. The rockface trembled. The guards closed ranks in terror. Breathless, Thoric saw the tongue shoot out of the gigantic mouth and crack like a whip in the middle of the room—very close to the Prince, who backed away, eyes ablaze although pale of face.

"Ah, my sweetheart," he murmured, "I bring you a lover . . . a barbarian from the south." He took a step closer. Once more the tongue snaked out, not more than the thickness of a knife-blade separating its tip from the Prince's chest. Thoric looked on in fascination as HalJin moved even closer, and the tongue slid over his clothes with a rustling sound—seeking something to latch onto. The Prince gave a little laugh and stepped back.

"Chain him!" he ordered the sentries.

Despite his struggles, they fastened Thoric's arms and legs with chains, and pulled them through iron rings in the wall. Arms high above his head and bare back pressed against the rough rockface, he hung there facing the creature. He was out of its reach—but he knew that it would not stay that way. He would meet his end between those mighty jaws. He could see bones and dark bloodstains on the floor in the middle of the room, and he knew that he would not be the beast's first victim.

Merely the next one!

He gritted his teeth. HalJin came over to him. He gave the guards a signal and they left the room with all speed. He undid the barbarian's belt and pulled his trousers down. The latter was now completely naked. With one eye on the barbarian's tense, muscular body, HalJin's voice had a note of mockery in it. "It is too early yet for carnal love. Your souls must first meet. Look at one another

. . . look at one another. . . ." He let out a shrill laugh and strode off toward the door, his gaze switching from monster to victim and back. Then he disappeared through the door, and there came the grating noise of the bolt being pushed home.

Thoric could feel the terror creeping over him. The reptile's gaze came to rest on him, and remained fixed there.

# 12

"Ah! SaiTeh." HalJin motioned to the minstrel to come over to him, and stared at him thoughtfully. "I should like to hear it again!"

SaiTeh nodded, relieved. The fate of the blond barbarian filled him with horror to the very depths of his soul, and to be ordered to sing chased away from the surface of his consciousness, at least for a while, all his thoughts on the uncertainty of life in the courts of princes. He sang the ballad again—if anything, perhaps, even a little more impressively than before, because horror is most clearly expressed when one feels some of it oneself. When he had finished, HalJin leaped to his feet and paced up and down uneasily. He spun round unexpectedly: "Sing me the part again, where it goes: 'The heavens were rent asunder and the rotting bodies of the dead came pouring down.' "

Once more the musician repeated the climax of the story. He thought he saw HalJin's face become still paler as the last notes rang out.

"Tanilorn," murmured the Prince. "Are you familiar with that barbarian land?"

SaiTeh shook his head. "No, my Prince. I have never traveled that far south."

"Yes, it is in the south," murmured HalJin softly, "in the south. . . ." He slumped back in the throne. "Could it be. . . ?" he whispered softly to himself, without finishing the sentence. Then he gave a violent shake of his head. "This is stupid! If it were so the wizard would have known of it. Many would know of it!" No, the Tanilorner had to die, and now.

He rose to his feet. Only old fools sat brooding.

"ChuenGoch!" he cried, gesturing to the musician to stand aside.

However, it was not the commander of the bodyguard who came striding into the Prince's private audience chamber; it was the commandant of the midnight patrol. His round face was white, and HalJin had the sudden sensation that danger was lurking. However the Prince concealed his feeling behind a mask of unfriendliness.

"My Prince!" cried the commandant, bowing hastily in front of the throne.

"I might easily have been asleep at this time, Commandant . . ." began HalJin.

"And it is thanks to men such as I that you are able to do so," interrupted the latter.

"The opposite would seem rather to be the case," growled the Prince.

"Listen to me!" the guard commander interjected once more. "Demons are attempting to break into the palace!"

"What are you saying?" HalJin felt the blood drain from his features, and his hands began to tremble. "You are talking nonsense . . ." he said.

"I know what I am saying, Excellency."

"Your report!"

The commandant obeyed angrily. He realized instantly the effect that his story was having on the Prince, and his anger subsided a little, as a result of which his tale became somewhat more animated. The demons became even more horrific than had actually been the case, their onslaught bloodier, their shrieks more terrifying. The unknown sentry would be likely to tell a different story . . . but what of it? Did not demons appear in different forms to different people? So terror-laden was his voice that he himself trembled even more. The Prince's voice quavered when he asked the question, "How is it that you are still alive?"

For a moment the commandant wondered at it himself. Then he told the tale of his aide's wondrous weapon.

The first glimmer of disbelief appeared in the Prince's eye. His initial impulse to release the Tanilorner instantly and thus to deliver himself from the demon's fury withered away. A hesitant grin came to his lips. The commandant had been drinking. Anybody who saw pink elephants would certainly be susceptible to blue daggers! Or. . . ? Ha! The Gods take the rascal. "Commandant!" he began. "Need I remind you that your job is to command the midnight patrol, and not to go carousing in some inn!"

The door flew open and ChuenGoch came in. His cloak sparkled with the droplets left by melted snowflakes. Two guards followed him in, carrying a lifeless form—one of the patrol. They laid the motionless figure in front of the throne.

"We found him and three more like him in the guards' hut by the East gate. One of them is a kitchen-hand. The others are sentries. By the gate itself there are ten members of the midnight patrol lying in the snow."

"Ten?" cried the commandant.

" . . . and one whose face we do not know. He is dead, quite in contrast to the others," continued ChuenGoch.

HalJin slumped back in his throne out of shock and astonishment. All signs of doubt instantly vanished from his face. The guard commander had been telling the truth!

"Ten, did you say?" cried the commandant once more, as white as a ghost. "Then . . . then there is nobody left at the gate now," he stammered.

"Nobody," ChuenGoch affirmed. "I have already called up a replacement."

"They must already be in the palace by now," whispered the commandant, backing away from the others. "When I left to come and warn you, there were two men back at the gate."

"That means . . ." began ChuenGoch, taking a step nearer.

"Stay away from me!" cried the commandant, stepping back out of arm's reach of ChuenGoch.

"K'wan!" cried HalJin angrily, his voice wavering out of combined fear and fury. "Do you think that we. . . ?"

"They just look like you and me," replied the commandant, quaking in terror. "And we no longer have a blue dagger to tell which is which! Nobody can be sure any more!"

"Nonsense!" bellowed the Prince, who was convinced that he at least was no demon.

"Just look at him then," shouted the guard commander pointing at the lifeless form lying on the steps up to the throne. "Look closely at him, for he is one of them! Look at him! He is not dead! And nobody knows how long the spell will last!"

HalJin reached for his sword. "We shall kill him then!"

"A demon?" The commandant's laugh was shrill. "Kill a demon?"

"Silence!" roared the Prince, leaving his sword where it was. Although fear of demons, of the Undead, was firmly rooted in the Kanzany soul, HalJin was no coward. His corpulent being was governed by the spirit of a warrior. He bent over the motionless body, and felt the heart still beating. He felt the hot breath on his cold hand.

Suddenly the whole thing seemed like a joke. He wrenched his sword from its sheath and plunged it into the pale arm. That would prove once and for all whether the man was simply asleep or not! The point of the sword sank in, ripping open the flesh. The man did not wince—nor, indeed, did he make any movement at all. No groan issued from the half-open mouth, no blood oozed from the deep gash.

HalJin raised the point of the sword up to his disbelieving eyes. It was still clean and shiny!

"We must keep a cool head," he whispered.

"Ah! That is assuming we can keep our heads at all!" cried the commandant. "Whose head do you have in mind?" he said, gazing at the Prince.

"Take this idiot out!" he said motioning to ChuenGoch.

The latter went instantly to carry out the order, but the commandant backed away, screaming. He turned and fled from the room, slamming the heavy door behind him. The men heard a scraping noise, and his voice calling out to the guards. ChuenGoch was the first to reach the door and tried in vain to open it. He threw himself against it with all his might, but the door withstood all his efforts. He turned and shrugged helplessly. "We are locked in," he said softly.

The Prince came running to his aid and they tried once more together. In vain. They banged on the door, but nobody came to open it. Nobody seemed to hear them at all.

"Where are your men, ChuenGoch—outside?"

ChuenGoch shook his head. "On the staircase."

"K'wan! So nobody will hear us," he laughed suddenly. "Locked in by my own patrol!" He shook his head.

"If that lunatic manages to convince your men that there are demons in here all our banging and shouting will only strengthen their conviction." He stepped back from the door.

A smile crept over ChuenGoch's narrow lips. "His white face alone will be enough to convince at least half of them," he said.

HalJin broke into a grin, cheered by ChuenGoch's smile. "And the pale faces of that half will surely convince the rest. My friend, we are victims of tradition and legend. Even if there are no demons in the palace, there is assuredly one sweeping through the night out there like a hurricane; the ancient fear in our people—and fear is the most evil spirit of all. I can feel it myself." The grin died on his lips.

"Do you really think . . . ?" began ChuenGoch.

HalJin motioned to him to be silent. "I do not know what I think. Uncertainty is just as evil as fear." His gaze came to rest on his minstrel who was sitting in a corner, white-faced and silent. "What do you think, SaiTeh?"

ger. SaiTeh had a sudden desire to run off and join the others outside. He heaved a sigh and pressed himself to the wall. The Prince walked over to him, wrenched the lute from his crooked fingers and smashed it on the ground. The strings resonated loudly round the room, drowning the sound of the wood splintering.

"You cannot even break dead objects without their crying out," said the minstrel softly, and his eyes took on a strange gleam as HalJin's face convulsed in rage. He knew that it was important to die rapidly now, or else it would be in an eternity of torment. "You are simply a cruel, fat animal," he whispered.

ChuenGoch's dagger flashed, but once more the Prince's hand intervened. "Let us not extinguish this surge of spirit. It will yet give me much to think about. And he has yet much to learn. . . ." He grasped the minstrel by the collar of his shirt and dragged him over to the window. "Those people down there, tomorrow they will come creeping back into the palace. All will be just as it was before, and I would miss you. Your absence would ever remind me of this moment of weakness." He let go, and the minstrel sank to the floor. "You will always be at my side. And now, I should like you to remain silent!"

SaiTeh heaved a sigh. Neither life nor death! But relief flooded over him as ChuenGoch placed the dagger back in his belt. Dying was not as easy as he had thought. Staying alive was easier.

"It has become very quiet," said HalJin suddenly.

All three of them held their breath and listened. There was not the slightest sound to be heard. An eerie silence filled the walls and rooms of the palace. The men had fled, and with them all the noise and bustle.

"We are alone here," stated ChuenGoch.

Then came the sudden noise of the wind singing as it came over the walls. A whistling noise streaked through the empty halls. Curtains fluttered in the audience chamber. The last candles on the stone steps went out and fell to the floor, still in their bronze holders, as the heavy drapes caught them. The great stone building was filled with metallic rustling noises, followed by the creaking of an open door. . . .

"Do you think. . . ?" said HalJin the hairs rising at the nape of his neck.

"It is merely the wind." Even ChuenGoch's voice sounded uncertain.

"Perhaps. . . ."

A sudden gust made the door rattle, and the chill of a snow-bound winter's night swept across the faces and arms of the three men.

HalJin drew his sword. "Whatever is out there, I do not intend to wait about in here doing nothing. Tear the curtains down from the windows and tie them together. The window is high and the walls are smooth, but we must try!"

Shocked, the three prisoners were suddenly feverishly active.

# 13

It felt to Thoric almost as if the reptile was deriving pleasure from his nakedness. It blinked at him in chill delight. However, he was inclined to view it as a simple sign of appetite. He rattled his chains to see how firmly they were attached. He might just as well have tried moving the wall itself. However, the rustling of the chains appeared to arouse the monster from its torpor. It raised its head and the tongue snaked across the room. Thoric felt its breath and jerked back, even though he knew the beast could not reach him. He shuddered as he gazed more deeply into the creature's jaws.

The vast reptile pushed its head up hard against the bars. Its tail lashed the air, hurling clouds of sand and dust and rotting straw up to the ceiling. It let out a roar, and Thoric tensed every muscle. The stakes in the cage, as thick as a man's arm, suddenly seemed frail and light. The tongue shot out once more and curled round one of the bars. A mighty jerk caused it to shudder. Dust and stones came crashing down from the ceiling—but the stake held.

Thoric looked on in bewilderment as his killer-to-be sank once more into a state of silent expectation, the cold reptilian eyes trained on the helpless victim.

He relaxed a trifle. He was still safe for a while. His gaze wandered over the row of bars in the fence. He could see no door. Therefore they would have to untie him and push him through one of the gaps between them—or else simply bring him nearer the cage, when the tongue would do the rest. That would be the moment to make his effort. Until then he could do only the same as the monster—wait!

He had lost all sense of time, and had no idea of how long he had been in this room. Lady Death was making him wait for her.

Thoric's thoughts roamed freely about over his memories, but always returned to TayaSar, whose odd little smile and teasing gaze would not leave his inner eye any more readily than would the image of the moment when the clothes had slipped from her body.

The torch had almost burnt right down when he thought he heard steps. There could be no doubt about it—the reptile raised its head and its eyes shone as it too stared toward the entrance.

The door opened, and Thoric let himself go completely limp. He hung there in his chains, ready to marshal all his strength at the decisive moment. Bright torchlight danced across the floor of the now almost pitch-black room, illuminating the faces of the Prince and ChuenGoch. They were red with effort, and their hair was damp from the snow. Somebody else slipped into the room behind them, and Thoric recognized the minstrel. A smile came to his lips. Were they intending an accompaniment of songs and music as he went to his death?

The reptile raised itself up high. The room shuddered. HalJin took the guttering torch from its emplacement near the prisoner and affixed a new one in its stead. Then he stared into the expressionless face of his prisoner.

"I should like you to tell me where you have taken the girl." He smiled at Thoric's silence. "Understand this, and understand it well. It is not so much for the sake of the girl. . . ." His smile broadened. "If your honor as a southerner demands it, allow me to forego my ancient right and offer the gift of her virginity."

Since the prisoner made no reply, he went on. "However, I have the feeling that my little sister has also sought refuge." He shook his head, obviously saddened by Thoric's continued silence. "No?" He shrugged his shoulders. "Very well. You are right. What concern of yours are my family problems?"

What was that supposed to mean? Thoric could almost have shaken his head. Were they trying to confuse him with this idiotic babbling? Anything was possible. It had never been very clear to him what went on inside the heads of these poeple from the east.

"I shall put it down to the passion in your southern soul that you dared to try and enter the White Tower to free your loved one. That was a truly noble and heroic deed which I do not wish to crown with such an ending." So saying, he pointed to the huge saurian, which was obviously feeling that too much talking had been done already, for it rose up with a roar and crashed against the fence, causing a hail of stones to rain down on the men.

SaiTeh ventured to tap the Prince on the shoulder. "We would do well to hurry," he whispered.

"You are right, minstrel. But our friend here has to understand that we are setting him free out of respect for his courage," (*and not because we are so damned terrified*, he added under his breath). *He may not even know that the Dead are helping him,* he thought. *Perhaps this is all some mad illness. But I must be free of this business, and I need something to toss to my followers as a decoy, something that will make them feel that* I *am the only demon in this house!*

*They are setting me free?* Thoric was totally confused. He broke into a grin. *Hah! You will not use me as your plaything, you Kanzany rat!*

"I hope you will forgive me my little joke here, but you should realize that nobody gets into my palace and tries to rob me without some form of punishment. And I shall kill you if ever you try it again."

He gestured to ChuenGoch and the minstrel. "Release him!"

Thoric no longer understood any of this. He got ready to make his escape bid. The moment was nigh. Let them talk. As soon as his fetters were off. . . .

The two men wrestled with his chains, and tried to release them from the rings with their daggers.

"You should know that our blacksmith is not to hand just at the moment . . . these are . . . unusual times," declared the Prince.

The men succeeded in releasing the chains that attached his arms above his head. Thoric remained still until they had also released the fetters round his ankles. Then he tensed himself and sprang!

ChuenGoch and SaiTeh were knocked aside in a flash. HalJin, however, despite his corpulence, skipped nimbly to one side. Thoric made an arc through the air since his trousers were still round his ankles, hampering his ability to run.

These violent goings-on spurred the monster on to renewed attacks on the bars of its cage. Its tongue rasped across the stony ground and encircled the arm of the Tanilorner, now lying in the middle of the room, his hands still tied.

HalJin let out a cry. Fate seemed determined to frustrate his plans, as if she intended to find out once and for all whether demons really would come to avenge the death of the barbarian—precisely the truth the revelation of which HalJin had judged too risky to contemplate. He wrenched the sword from his belt.

ChuenGoch rushed toward Thoric to hold him down. The reptile's tongue gave a jerk, dragging the two powerfully built men nearer to the bars. The beast tried to encircle both of them with its tongue at the same time.

SaiTeh seized the commander of the bodyguard by the leg and pulled with all his might. For an instant it looked as though all three of them would be dragged between the bars of the cage. Then HalJin awoke from his stupor. His sword came down, scything through the muscular tongue. The reptile let out a great bellow, and hurled itself against the bars, reaching out in vain with the stump of its tongue. The men stumbled backwards, gasping with the effort of pulling Thoric with them.

"Quickly!" urged SaiTeh, hurling the door open. "Quickly you fools!"

In a hail of stones and dust, and to the accompaniment of a roar which caused the very walls to shake, they dashed from the room. Heaving a mighty sigh of relief, HalJin shot the bolt home.

SaiTeh surveyed it anxiously.

"Have no fear," gasped HalJin, "this entrance is too narrow for the monster." A smile set in as he continued, "And it is the only way out of the room."

"How did the beast get in there, then?" asked SaiTeh in surprise.

"It was born in there." HalJin turned to the Tanilorner, who was totally bewildered. "Tonight you shall be my guest, Southerner. The ambassador from Famtomsekapok has departed suddenly. You will have to make do with his chambers."

# 14

The Kanzany mind is just as bent as the Kanzany sword, thought Thoric as he left the palace. You can never be sure what they will dream up next! He shook his head. He cast an occasional glance over his shoulder, but there was nobody following him, which inspired him to further head-shaking. Sometimes he would stop suddenly to listen, but he heard no telltale noises of snow crunching underfoot. Was the Prince really not having him followed? Did he really no longer have any interest in finding out where the Princess was hidden? Perhaps he knew already?

Then it struck him that there had been no guards at the gate. Indeed, more than that, he had encountered not a soul on his way through the palace and courtyard. Therefore nobody but the Prince, the guard commander and the minstrel knew that he had been released! What devilment was this? What plot had the unfathomable mind of the Prince hatched?

He shook himself down and strode out more boldly. Nothing was going to make him spend the rest of the night in the palace. No, that would be stretching his good fortune too far. He was sufficiently familiar with the inconstancy of the Kanzany mind, but Prince HalJin surpassed by far anything or anybody he had ever previously encountered.

His grin broadened further at the thought of the eagerness with which the three men had helped him search for his sword in the snow-covered courtyard. He had certainly never gone grubbing about in the snow with a Prince before.

When he reached the first houses in the town he turned round again. The palace still appeared totally dead.

The town was fast asleep too. He reached Sas-Kan's house unchallenged, but he had to knock several times on the door before anybody came to open it. On his bed he found a pouch full of gold. Inside it there was an accompanying sheet of parchment on which were written the words

"THORIC! IF YOU ARE STILL ALIVE, TAKE THIS GOLD WITH MY ETERNAL THANKS. THE PRINCESS IS IN A SAFE HIDING PLACE!"

# 15

He smiled and closed the pouch, weighing it thoughtfully in his hand.

TayaSar. . . .

She would be in need of his help to get away from the city. The streets were snowbound and dangerous.

He attached the pouch to his belt, lost in thought. No, it was time for him to vanish, and quickly at that. Let the merchant worry about the girl. HalJin was a madman, and his sort were to be trusted as little as possible. He might already have changed his mind and be after him again!

He had to find another way of reaching TrondasKhyn. The sorcerer did not appear to be in the city. If he were to stay, and the sorcerer returned, then he might get to know him, but it was a risky proposition.

There had to be another way—after all, he had a sword and gold now!

Once more his thoughts wandered to the person

of TayaSar. His horse came to a halt and stood there, stamping impatiently.

He pulled himself together with a jerk and turned his back on the town. A few minutes later, he was riding along the snow-covered road leading between the embattled walls and out into the open country.

It had stopped snowing. The air was cold and frosty, and at his back the first glimmers of dawn were creeping across the sky.

Here too there was already talk of war. It seemed that there was some truth in the prophesies of the fortune-tellers. He dismissed the thought from his mind, but it was not easy. War was not to his liking. He might all too easily get caught between two fronts.

Perhaps he should postpone his search for TrondasKhyn and try to learn more about this damned war. For that he would need to leave the wintry highlands.

A horse snorted, arousing him from his thoughtful reverie.

A rider appeared at his side, wearing a dark cloak and a Kanzany fur hat.

Thoric's hand flew to his sword, but he left the weapon in its sheath when he saw the long hair and pale face.

"I was watching SasKan's house," said TayaSar breathlessly. "I am glad you escaped my brother's clutches!"